The Infinite Mind of Lio'lf

Pronunciation- [Lah-If]

The Infinite Mind of Lio'lf © 2020 Carlos V. Kaigler

Printed in the United States of America

Cover & Interior Design: Carlos V. Kaigler /C'vaughn'K Graphic Designs/ The Poet B.GKL

ISBN-13: 978-0-578-80322-7

Website:
www.authorbgkl.com

Sites:
https://linktr.ee/Thepoet_BrothaGKL
https://linktr.ee/MrAndMrsKaigler
https://linktr.ee/CvaughnKphotography

Email:
Thepoet-b.gkl@hotmail.com

Business:
C'vaughn'K Graphic Designs
(313) 334-9630

Melvin Johnson

PRESTIGIOUS ART COLLECTION ™

Rest In Peace
December 29, 1953 - April 6, 2020

I wanted to occasionally place some of Mr. Melvin Johnson's drawings throughout parts of my book to show my respect to him, and his impressive work; with the approval of his wife and my wonderful mother-in-law Mrs. Ruth Dianne Johnson with honoring me the permission to use his art. Melvin Johnson was a 66-year-old veteran of the United States Navy and a retired officer for the Detroit Police Department with many other achievements. Melvin Johnson also self-taught himself a skill to create memories by finding time to master his craft of drawing, and creating abstract sculptures of magnificence to leave for many eyes to see. After transcending, and leaving a legacy behind for his wonderful family to honor while motivating them to also value their skill to master anything in life. Now embrace some of the many great pieces from the *Melvin Johnson Prestigious Art Collection*.

Acknowledgments

I would like to dedicate my first book to the energy of what writing is as a craft, by respecting the poetic spoken word of emotions that always kept me grounded by writing my mind as I see fit like therapy. I would also like to give thanks to certain people that I trust and truly love, that helped me along the way in my personal life to be able to focus on my growth. There wouldn't be any true poetry or writing within me without the love of my *Aunt and Author Deborah Wright*, for always sitting down to show me how to format my thoughts into writing while in my early stages, which also motivated me to master my craft further on my own.

Mastering ways to express a deeper style of love, happiness, anger, pain, and more as well as the imagination of developing my thoughts in a classy but realistic manner. I love and thank my beautiful royal love my wife *Charnissa V. Kaigler* for supporting my craft down to helping me brainstorm for my book title, buying writing supplies, giving endless support as well as paying into my dream, and being my light. My wife arranged and scheduled my first and second live poetry readings; my wife has done more than I could ever explain with words to express my ultimate love and loyalty upon her walk while changing my life. Also, my awesome love goes to someone special I adopted into my heart as my big sister... *Sal Wilcher*, just for loving me and allowing me to perform on her band time and showing up for my first and second performance with powerful love; she is always so deep with her love and I embrace that for life.

The great legend *James Earl Jones* was one of my biggest inspirations for so many things I value doing today. Things such as narrating, acting, poetry, and writing. I honored the way he brings all words and roles to life by just speaking from the strength of his voice; he encouraged me to dig deeper as well as left gems in his awesome books I enjoy learning from... I thank you sir for just being you.

My skills in my life were motivated by things I have seen or learned from my aunts and uncles, my talented *Aunties Deborah* and

Patricia, and my talented *Uncles Bernard* and *Danny*. I have collected many skills by watching or learning many things from what they were willing to teach me personally.

Aunt and Author Deborah Wright: Actress, Poet, Writer, Singer, and Hip Hop Artist... I want to thank you for being there for me and nurturing the broken parts of my heart and allowing me to speak without judgment; you were always like a mother to me and still until this day, I thank you for never giving up on me and I love you for that and much more.

Uncle Bernard/Legacy Blake: Actor, Singer, Writer, Sketch Artist... I want to thank you for being more than an uncle to me all my life, you were always like a father to me and more; such a deep mind you have with so many things to offer. You prepped my style of being a classy gentleman and teaching me the sounds of instruments while schooling me on classy music and art; I appreciate you for hearing me speak my heart for hours while just listening and then healing my words and I love you for that and much more.

Aunt Patricia/Gavierredesign: Seamstress/Custom Designer, Singer, and Sketch Artist... I want to thank you for reading awesome books to me as a child which helped advance my story-writing skills, and mindset while also being a strong ear for what I had to say; you have been in the shadows helping me with so many things that could have stopped me from continuing life or making my life harder and I love you for that and much more.

Uncle Danny/Young Juicy: Actor, Hip Hop, and R&B Artist, Writer, Dancer... I want to thank you for just being the energy I needed to see, I always honored your drive to never give up on what you love no matter what happens, and I wanted to gain that same type of confidence one day and I did so; Sometimes just watching someone can build the soul to work harder, I watched you rehearse songs and moves for hours on in towards perfection. I noticed your glow, and I love you for that and much more.

Rest in Power to My father *Carlos V. Kaigler Senior*, and rest with knowing I never stopped writing after you told me you were proud of my work… along with telling me to do the right thing; you always told me you love me always, and I shall be that way to others that love me the same way. I shall always value the hard work you placed in my soul and I love you and miss you always.

I want to thank my awesome stepmother *Rosalyn* for marrying my dad and being a great mom, best friend, and more. One of the things you always did that I truly needed… was just listening to my heart when I needed to escape my world and just regroup from my mistakes or just wanted to laugh. I never considered you as just a stepmother but an awesome mom that embraces me fully as a son as I honor you as a mother… I love you always.

I want to thank my three beautiful children my son and two daughters for being the reason I started changing my surroundings, and taking this world more seriously while molding my life craft to be a better me for the future of all three of my children… I love you to life.

Granny T, I want to thank you for seeing my talent, and always trying to refine my skills by reading the dictionary or learning arts and crafts; telling me you love me from the core and more while loving my mind and making me the center and traveling the map. *Grand Mama Wright* for just teaching me blues and telling me the truth with love and allowing me to crash at your house when things got hard, and also just being so easy to talk to… I love you both.

I want to thank my mom *Cynthia J.W.,* for always showing me what hard work looked like, and for being a strong provider and powerful woman at all times along with other things I may have valued; thank you for appreciating my poetry when I called your voice mail or just wrote it with love. May my *great grandmother* rest in power with serenity and also thinking her beautiful soul for helping you a lot with us growing up along with some of the family now and then. Moms I always give credit where it's deserved always, I honored your strength, and I take that to the grave with love.

Sending my powerful love to all of my wonderful biological little Sisters and brothers... *Rico aka Ram Keenng, Latoya, Jazzy, Trionne, Brittany aka Toonie, Alexis M.K. aka Lexy, Taylor, Javonte, Javaughn,* I love you all to life.

I want to embrace and spread my Infinite love to my magnificent new in-laws that I consider more than just in-laws, my *Mother Love Mrs. Ruth Dianne Johnson, Pop Big Ken, Big Sister* & *Author Charise,* and her awesome sons/my new nephews *Zion* and *CJ, Ivanique Williams...* I love you all and can't wait to see the memories we make as a family.

I want to give love and thanks to all the people I hold close to me. The ones that gave me a lot of motivational reasons to keep pursuing my goals, along with being patient with my growth. I love you all with my soul and heart, regardless if we are not related by blood, I honor the love given every day.

Special thanks for getting my book done and more: *Best-Selling Author Dr. Patricia Demps* for becoming an awesome big sister and best friend in my life and helping me with a lot of business and book information I needed to finish my manuscript process towards its publishing, and being in my corner with true family love with support and more. *Best-Selling Author Kamal Lukata* for being an awesome brother and helping with what I needed towards getting this book in order, with awesome information towards the middle of my book, love you both family.

Thank You *Jah Knowa* for coming into my life and being a big brother to me, and always giving me knowledge upon what I already gained on my own, love you, my family. Thank you *Ebony Neco Washington* for being an awesome sister and allowing me to perform on stage on your time... love you always. There are just too many wonderful people to thank all at once; I am showing love to the people that I have gained as a family just from social media and in life. You know who you are, and I honor our family ship forever.

"We should never live to die we must live to live."
Sincerely, Carlos "*The Poet B.GKL*" Kaigler
Peace & Love…

The Infinite Mind of Lio'lf

Pronunciation- [Lah-If]

Carlos *"The Poet B.GKL"* Kaigler

Lio'lf *[Lah-If]*

- The combination of two wild strengths becoming one. A lion and wolf. As a king of my pride, and a leader of my pack. I am *the infinite mind of Lio'lf.*

"Life is a choice & death is not an option"

Sincerely, *The Poet B.GKL/Brotha GKL/Gawd Keenng Lio'lf*

CONTENTS

#684

Her Love for the Blues...
The Hole in the Wall
Chapter 1

Episode 1: **Spontaneous Midnight**

Wake up sweet darling.
I need to take you somewhere.
Hidden deep in the Mississippi swamps.

Held far in the mossy greenwoods.
I know it's late… but don't worry your lips.
Just rise, and wear that blue dress that I like.

Don't wear any shoes at all… I rather carry you.
(Just trust me.)

They say!
3 AM is the best time, to be at this place.
Let's lose ourselves, and fade away into the fog.

Just hold my neck, and faint against my heartrate.
Past the snakes, gators, and weeping trees.

Slight sounds of dirty blues, holding the air captive.

To Be Continued...

Episode 2: **Swamp Lust**

Holding her voluptuous curiosity, against the sweat of my broken shirt.
Earth surrounds my bare walk through the green, the brown of nature, and the moistness of its firmament.

Permanent frequencies of blues getting closer, but so damn far and truly needed.
Completed steps of desires on our breath as she looks up at my five o'clock throat, and oily beard.

Veered by thoughts of her, kissing the corn liquor drips from my corner lips.
Ripped jeans flirting with the swamp breeze, passing through the stride of my bones.

Stones playing ruff with the soul of my hill, with the compliments of her energy on me.

See her eye's in the red moon as the faint sound of blues pulls us closer to the hole in the wall.

All this candy in my arms, blue dress squeezed tight against the back of her legs above the hold of my forearm.

Turned slowly near an old tree and whispered, let's stop here for a moment; were a mile from the juke joint.

She asked why! And I replied.
Because I got the blues darling.

To Be Continued...

Episode 3: **Become the Moss**
Yoni: /yoh-nee/ *the essence of women's universal life-giver and love.*
Gawddess: /ˈɡɑː.des/ *Infinite goddess form of a Kween aka Queen in power.*

She repeated back to me sensually… Oh, the blues huh!
I replied yes, but not the kind of storm that lingers above the crown
of our head sweetheart.

Art of blues that allows this old bitter tree, to be our welcome
center.
Enter this moment as we lay against the broken roots, and sticky
leaves.

Ease your soul upon my humid climate, and spread your soft
fingertips.

Chips of wood, and rocks engraved on my back with her shadow
upon me.

Free your frustrations, and challenge your eyes to stay focus.
Surface your random movements, and release your yoni's delicious
sage.

Enslave my hands with your bosom and rib cage, while reading my
palms.
Songs played by the howling wolf, creeping up her body as she
swallows the vibrations of the live band.

Hands of her hunger… buried in the pit of my chest; scatting with
her joints.
Points of her bust motivate our next enchanting's of reason.

Even thus the nights are gritty but alluring… yet so captivating!
Eliminating her control and placing the submission of her power
upon the rule of my single empire.

Vampire kisses down the stretch marks bestowed upon her flower-
like skin, and southern mass.

Flask of black liquor flooded across the moisture… down her landscape of forest and rain.

Games of darkness fill the swamp with banshee shrieks and sweet howling romance.

Dance of true blues embracing our inebriated beauty.
Truly thrust, the blue dress around her waist like a halo.
Slowly, she whispered… feeling the guitar strings in her legs that cry.

I held her to melt, and she **1, 2, 3**; and I **4, 5, 6.**
Gifts are given as the stars blow out the way we ignite.

Right now this is beautiful I breathed slowly to her, but let's make it to the hole in the wall.

Involved, withholds of her loitering grip around the V cut of my rhythm and candle-like sweat.

Chest against her panting and my endeavors to inner stand her muttering spells of raunchy energy.

Penalties of her flesh grinding and stealing my essence as we release the relief.
Breathed in, and got dressed to continue the walk with my Gawddess… in my arms.

To Be Continued...

Episode 4: **Blues Dripping From the Ceiling**

Burns of blues forcing us towards a filled porch of drunken fedora hats, and flirting gardenia flowered damsels.

Mantels of throats releasing cigar smoke, from their suited pit as silk dresses are brushed above the knee with appetites.

Lights of two single lanterns holding the sides of this wooden jukebox of blues, and sweaty skin.

Grins of later on bed-hopping and pimp line pinching, on the loose wooded dance floor shifting.

Twisting hips and guitar runs and riffs, provoking the cognac's feel into all empty glasses for sober tongues.

Guns attached to the rib cages and all ankles of players rolling sevens in the corner of the hole in the wall against the borders.

Orders are taken by a Skirt high barefooted southern pie, bringing spirits to the blues on stage taking a 3-minute break.

Wait! My wife whispered slowly in worry about the scene with us both standing at the steps of this hot gritty and dark.

Start looking in her mind of worries, and calmed her with lips upon her neck and down to the shoulders of her blue dress.

Confess to me your fears of good old back wood blues my dear, and I shall give light to which you are frightened of.

Love if you don't feel comfortable here, I shall carry you through all of where we came from with no anger.

Strangers cut eyes from the shadowed parts of the balcony, as a beautiful old woman leaned forward and spoke wisely.

(I's be Mrs. Down Home Suga, you all can call me Momma Biggs, and this here is my Swamp house of blues.
Use-Them-their steps and go in, Momma Biggs is not gone let nothing happen to you baby sweets, don't be afraid of what-cha see out here child.)

While we thanked Momma Biggs, my wife clinched my waist and walked slowly as her soft bare feet walk.

Talk of mumbling and intoxicating compliments are made by the yellow eyes in the dice corner with harsh lust and intent.

The scent of warm cotton candy flees from the barefooted waitresses; slithering through the corn liquored bodies.

Knotty gestures of dirty dancing in our eyes, as my wife's shoulders become to loosen up and legs begin bending.

Ascending rhythms of blues begin to climb through her like possessions of root work with the energy of melanin coffee.

Softly taken over by the drum snares in her heart, thee electric guitar strings in her veins, becoming a vessel for blues.

Rules of the house are to lose ourselves and become slaves to the sounds of the night strings plucked.

Suck thee atoms of my apple and press your gentle jam of legs together and dance your soul upon me.

Honey! She replied, this would be a perfect time for a whiskey on the rocks; I replied, but you don't drink whiskey.

Tipsy as I feel, by the blues she says; I want spirits poured on my body and drunken from the cleavage of my heart.

Start with my back first she's said and let it run down the wisdom of my spine to the movement of my rapture.

Master of our moment, the room is in a complete trance and has no cares of our blues spell to arouse each other.

The color of the room begins to change like laced drinks, and people start to blur like tear-gassed eyes or funny smoke.

Dope like systems, as blues got louder and brown fragments of souls dancing with hands groping and naked eyes.

Rise of heat and the blues is pushing buttons; as dresses begin to fall against the sound of belt buckles releasing with hunger.

Thunder and rain started as water creeps through and drip on the dance floor of heat that was starting to grind and peek the meter.

Neither, I or my wife has ever seen such a party of naked souls in their world with blues.

Soothed and erotic air with sounds of women lusting after men and men lusting after women with moans.

To Be Continued...

Episode 5: **Mister Hellhound and Gold Ring**
Kween: /kwiːn/ *the truest form of the real Queen.*
Gawddess: /ˈgɑː.des/ *Infinite goddess form of a Kween aka Queen in power.*

Bones of dominoes, slapping down on a shabby hard table of third legs and berretta leathered holsters.
Coasters are non-existent in this skeptical but erotic blue's parlay of hounds and dames.

Strange contingencies of feelings that this place is held under a compelling dominion of tantric blues.

Virtues of necromancy, charming from the tapping rings I have seen; beyond my **Kween's** perspirating bouncing shoulder.

Colder paranoia distracts my peripheral of an old string plucker; I overheard being called Mister Hellhound.

Crowned with a Dobb, that had better days with a black guitar with cigar smolder descending.

Offending yellow eyes, towards the curvy size of my wife dancing and grinding.

Unwinding her body to the inducement of blues, but blind to the ignorance of Mister Hellhound and his hooligan's corner.

Mourner I shall be without the grief if this buffoon keeps gawking at my lady. Baby, I think we may have a problem; I whispered angered in my wife's drum while she presses to me.

I agree she replies, without causing any attention and voiced that she's been ignoring this crude man.

Band of blues playing muffled, as my awareness and defense start to surge.

Purge and darkness take my heart and reigns over my rational way of being a gentleman by far.

Bizarre smoke comes from the smoke of his soggy stogie concealed in his seared jaw.

Withdraw of discomfort leaking from my Gawddess while the feelings of insidious caution to keep me on edge.

Pledge of nobleness allows my legs to walk before making a cunning decision of evading the trap.

Back turned on my wife to vanquish this wooden chair hustler and low-level gunslingers.

Fingers across my right bicep; wife holding me, screaming wait! While the blues never stop.

Hilltop backward hole-in-the-wall… is about to feel my cognition and magnitude.

Chewed baccy went into a halt, sundress waiters have become absent; the busty bartender started mixing slower.

Viola! The barmaid whispered, go get Mama Biggs; this shit is about to get foolish.

The clueless local motion toward Mister Hellhound and his loosely clutched guitar and shady persuasion.

The occasion of dancing vessels standstill with horrified glares upon their faces.

Aces of a full hand dropped and dice played its last set of sevens while my wife tries to prevent warfare.

A flare of candles blown by eerie wings to a window behind his seat.
The heat of fire hit my third eye, from the flick of his last puff and then I blinked.

A wink towards my wife from the stage, as Mister Hellhound played after vanishing before me in smoke.

I hope this isn't the voodoo blues player I heard swamp stories about.
A shout of raw blues screams melodious, but menacing tones drove the room back into hypnosis.

Psychosis sets in, as my wife floats towards his trickery and Momma Biggs stands door side at my confusion.

Losing my mind while the Hellhound plays his dark chords with amusement.

To Be Continued...

Episode 6: **The Grievous, Subdue Of Strain**

Kween: /kwiːn/ *The truest form of the real Queen.*
Yoni: /yoh-nee/ *the essence of women's universal life-giver and love.*

Translucent radiance… starts to render from his shady strings, while the toes of my wife's feet hover above the stumped buds and spilled booze.

Shoes of all the fools in the blues room moving aside, watching my Kween be taken by the conjuration of this unearthly instrument panderer.

The handler of souls I yelled! You will not take my Vernita away from me with your ritual of enticement and mental infliction.

The friction of his lackeys begins to brew while stepping forth, as my voice altered the entire gin mill of midnight people of the wetland.

Damn, I whispered! While my wife is still being pulled towards the stage under Mister Hellhound's guitar strings unloaded.

{Hold it, fellas, I'll take it from here… it seems that Mama Biggs didn't tell this boy, who owns the land of this place that we are standing.

Handing out thee acceptance into the hole in the wall is Mama Bigg's place and power to do so, but the soil of dirt it sits on is my playground.}

The sound of my voice felt like I was muted or silenced by his dark spell, while every muscle in my body felt too dead to move while he spoke.

{Oak wood and the moaning voices of women is what my guitar is made of, so whatever the Hellhound wants… will damn shore be given.

Driven by the crossroads and the bleeding liquor in my bloody Mary's and all the succulent Yoni that I chose for my harem of deeds.

Needs of your sweet Vernita, and the love you value of her; shall soon end and she will only sing the blues on her knee's beneath me.}

Freely I thought to myself, break the restraints, and use every obstacle of pain towards the stage of his sliced grinning face.

Then a fireplace explodes, when a waitress jerks away from a goon that wants to fondle her petite cuff and nipples; while shots of rum slam against the mantle.

Candle hits the floor and spreads more flames rapidly, while Mister Hellhound gets distracted; now I am released from his sorcery.

Forcefully I ran towards my wife like a stone on the water as the place is engulfed in a blaze; I embraced my Kween in midair.

From there I prepared myself to jump through a full glass window and never stop running, while my wife tries to shake off the weird trance.

Dance of burning bodies jumping into the gator-infested swamp, trying to relieve themselves of the smoke and orange singe.

Revenge in Mister Hellhound's eyes as he stands inside the fueling hole in the wall, with insane hate coming from behind the broken window… just snarling.

Darling everything is going to be fine, as I held her tight against my shredded shirt and she whispered; *baby I can feel him coming for us.*

Ambitious but impossible… baby how the hell would you even know that?

She reacts and replies… *my love.*

Because his hat is on your crown and I can hear the hellhounds growling behind us, and she fainted and the hat caught fire and blew off my head.

Led by anger and misunderstanding, I ran faster with the sound of the wild beast behind me; but I chose not to look.

Shook with fear by a single plucked tone in the humid wind, followed by this voice… **{Mister Hellhound is coming to get what is needed… so run… because my blues always tales the last story... O that sweet Vernita smell}** {followed by his *Sinister Laugh*}

To Be Continued...

Episode 7: **Canine Cravings for Vernita**
Kween: /kwiːn/ *The truest form of the real Queen.*

Hellhound you can chase me Intel the skin of my shoes is raw, and the crease of my slacks begins to lose its entire meaning!

While leaning and limping from miles of running and intervening the mental take of my wife's mind from the blues dog.

Bullfrogs and creatures of the crescent night begin to sing louder, as Mister Hellhounds raspy utter gets more tamed.

Defamed I'm sure! For the distant smell coming from the hole in the wall inflamed and nearly in ashes, on behalf of Viola's discomfort with the outlaw.

An overdraw of bullets and bar fights heard over the yelling of Mama Biggs and her shotgun cracking to the jaw of the perverted hoodlum's mind.

All behind me it shall stay, as I aligned my vision and held her tighter while running past the snake fields and the possum forest of mud.

Blood drips on her cherry tattooed bosom, from the broken shards of glass in my shoulders and sliced chest.

I guess at some point, I have to stop and rest; while feeling her soft breath, as it cools my neck; while she's pent to my trotting body.

Probably I should stop soon, I can finally hear fewer sounds of blues, and that smell of mongrel drool; filling the fog with the stench of retaliation.

Aching lungs and fatigue sweat falling from my elbows and face; I feel like I'm about to lose all control and drop from the blood loss.

Cost of a good time turned into a war for greed and disrespect no man or thing shall break us apart, nor by music or dark tricks.

I feel sick Vernita, I have to stop and lie you down here baby; as I kneeled feeling drained but alert… looking down at my fainted wife.

Right before I kissed her, the heat from a chewed half-lit stogie; burns my face and is followed by the teeth of a hound on my hip.

Grip from one rusty musician's hand, holding my throat in the sky as Mister Hellhound just stared through my soul with the weirdest black and metallic eyes.

Paralyzed by the miles ran and the wounds gained, well my wife sleeps under a spell of dark body blues and cant rise, but yet the voice of this odd man arrives.

{Baptized within the smoke of my hate, and drowned in the pit of my guitar screams; got damn it, I told you, that your woman is already mine.}

Lifeline fading as Mister Hellhound releases my neck, as blood runs from my wounds as I slowly fall.

All I could do was try to stand and protect my Kween, but the immense amount of pain delivered to my tired torso was inhumane.

Fuming with heinous hate, he takes the belly of his guitar and destroys it across my waist; casting a shriek from my inner core.

A lion's roar flows through the swamp as my broken body hits the ground again, while Mister Hellhound creeps close towards Vernita.

Neither of my legs will move, and my eyes won't stay open.

To Be Continued...

Episode 8: **Banshee Blues and Royal Tongues of Vengeance**

Joking and snickering deeply, as he walked towards my wife after paralyzing me while forced to watch his boot and one knee; slowly kneeling next to her with a smile of mastery with thirst.

He began to converse insidious blues notes quietly from his throat, right after spitting out his stogie; he opened one of her eyes, and then opened her mouth and then brown fumes poured from his passage.

Savage and unsteady jerking start to take over her body, reacting to the brown odor of nefarious smoke and melodic guitar riffs; overwhelming her will, while storming through her wind pipe and principal with combative control.

Placing his chokehold to her neck to maintain his ritual perfectly, with plans to take her internally away from me… my feeling is coming back to my upper body with my pelvis holding splinters from the guitars impact.

I tried to distract his focal point of devouring Vernita's state of mind, just by throwing a large piece of his broken guitar towards the shoulder… mainly the arm holding her neck straight; watching pieces just disperse on contact.

Inexact hit without the full feeling in my legs to truly force any sort of rescue attempts, but the hit at least allowed Mister Hellhound to halt; with homicidal eyes plotting further anguish towards my life as he stands drastically in delirium and annoyance.

Clairvoyance running through my aching body, hoping he would call his wild mutts to rip me apart; Mister Hellhound looked into the sky and sounded a ghastly whistle, which sent chills through the entire backwoods silencing every sound… except the hellhounds growl galloping near.

The clear assumption that his mutts would be his next move, as he looked back down grinning while turning around to finish my wife off with his spells, but my plan is risky but worth it.

With perfect timing as my legs regained most of my strength, with the rhythm of pain playing against my bones; when the hounds leaped towards me, I launched my body towards my wife and passed him kneeling… assuming that he wouldn't allow them to attack me near my wife.

Strife and anger are now brewing with disruption, as Mister Hellhound stands rapidly while turning and pulling out a rusty harmonica; he begins to blow one silent note, and all hounds start burning like scraps of newspaper.

With acres of mongrels forced into a sorcerers oblivion, thinking of another plan to stop Mister Hellhound; but he turned and looked at me and then appeared closer with his boot slammed in my hip of excruciation, as my wife trembled in sorcery a foot away.

In disarray, he stared at me just to say *(YOU ARE A SIMPLE PLAGUE OF PROBLEMS, BUT I AM THE PURGATORY OF YOUR CONSEQUENCES TO ADJUST YOUR DEFIANCE… TO TRY, AND SAVE WHICH IS NEITHER YOURS ANY LONGER BOY.)*

(YOU ANNOY MY INNER BLUES AND ALL I WANTED IS YOUR WIFE JUST BECAUSE I DO; BUT BEFORE THAT… LET ME SHOW YOU WHAT TO DO WITH YOUR LAST BREATH OF LIFE.)

Mister Hellhound steps back away from my hip to the center of the woods while using his fingernail to slice his tongue off, and then he threw it upon a dying tree; the tree began to descend into the ground holding his lingua as it bleeds.

While I precede to be confused and wounded all over trying to wake my wife to run without having any luck of her even being aware of any of this; Mister Hellhound oddly is not leaking one drop of blood anywhere, which didn't make sense even for him being whatever he might be.

It definitely doesn't take a Ph.D. to know that I might not survive this night of blues with my Vernita; this is all my fault; *(STOP YOUR WHISPERING, AND FORESEE MY NEW BLUES GUITAR FROM THE ROOTS, AND RIGHT ALONG WITH A NEW TONGUE TO FINISH THE CEREMONY OF CAGING HER MIND AS MY BUTTERFLY OF SUBJUGATION.)*

The expiration on my life is not yet a fact but nearly just a threat, by a coward with a violent set of strings; without your enchantments, you're just a greedy old musician with desires to achieve any woman by using the trance of your blues spells.

(WELL I GUESS THAT YOU THINK THAT YOU HAVE ME ALL FIGURED OUT, NOT EVEN CLOSE; AND I ALSO ENJOY INSULTS BECAUSE IT MAKES THE SKIN HARD AND RESILIENT.)

(NOW GATHER YOUR EARS, SO THAT THEY MAY BLEED OUT AS I PLAY THIS MUDDY NEW NOTE THAT ENTOMBS YOU AND UNWRAPS HER VIRTUOUS VOICE; THE TRUE ROYAL TONGUE OF BLUES, UNVEILED IN HOWLING SCREAMS.)

Before he plucks the cord with murder on his breath, my wife's eyes opened and released a scream and growl from the swamps of all living predators of gruesome intent.

Mister Hellhound froze baffled but convinced that my Vernita was under his thumb, even with an unfinished ceremony interrupted; as she hovers a foot from the soil with eyes like jars of pennies and her dress spiraling with her wind.

As she ascends with the feeling of compelling control, seeming far greater than Mister Hellhound's instrument of ruin as she doesn't recognize the issue just yet; but gaining her thoughts instantly, while the Hellhound looks particularly uneasy.

A sleazy look hits his vision as he balled his hand around the neck of his guitar, sensing a different presence than the brown vapors he placed inside her for obedience; I continued to look at my wife while dripping blood from wounds and cuts, as he tries to walk towards her plucking the same club hypnosis.

Not focused on me, I tried to stand up in front of her to keep him away regardless of her condition and his powerful rootwork; he quickly looks at me while in an unbothered walk forward and my rib cage starts to feel fire-like pains, while my mind wonders why am I not dead yet.

Then corvette like lights appeared in her eyes as if she were fully aware of our journey and the pain I am enduring to keep us safe with my beaten body against this blues of darkness; Mister Hellhound tried to finish his song of entrapment but was having a harder time connecting the dots of her being.

Just seeing the way she got angry and moved forward so fast before Mister Hellhound could even react; Vernita appeared in a swarm of butterflies and began to permanently take every command of gifts he self-achieved.

He tries to leave but couldn't gain any of his dark tricks to twist the mind of what he tried to enslave in her; strings became toneless and snapping, as he tries to speak but his new tongue is taken along with his surrendered tongue for his new guitar without paying for it with our lives.

Cries and screams are quietly heard from past victims being stuck in his forceful pluck of dominance, he tries to whistle for his canines but they lay to rest as paper from his greed; misunderstanding his call to them which is displaced with a missing tongue to signal his need.

Weeds begin to grow from his dripping body of self-suffering and becoming regular, my wife spoke harmful words to him before she fainted to the grass, **(Now experience the true blues of my union in which you tried to invade Mister Hellhound, you are now exiled from the craft of Rhythm and Blues; now you get to live, incapacitated.)**

I hesitated while in pain and crawled over to my wife, as the Hellhound looked impaired and babbling rubbish on his knees; surrounded by black weeds, growing from his ways.

I raised the head of Vernita, baby please wake up and say something to me; she smiled and whispered in my ear, **(baby next time let's just use the eight-track or the vinyl blues records honey)…** that's a deal, my love!

It was then two headlights that popped up from a road that wasn't there at first, it was another couple we saw at Mama Biggs spot but they left early; **(Sir, and Mam… you both look in need of a ride back to the city, you both look pretty banged up, I and my lady don't mind at all dropping you both off)** that's fine by us we thank you kindly.

(What about your drunken blues friend there on his knees blindly mumbling?)

Humbling concern, but he's no friend of ours, but I do believe he has a ride coming later.

Then I heard the teeth of a wild gator closing its jaws behind us, silencing the jabbering of Mister Hellhound's confusion; while kissing my wife on the temple, I swore I saw those weird lights in her eyes still as she fell to sleep on me… I guess I'm seeing things again.

A shot of gin would be nice right now… damn what a night!

11681

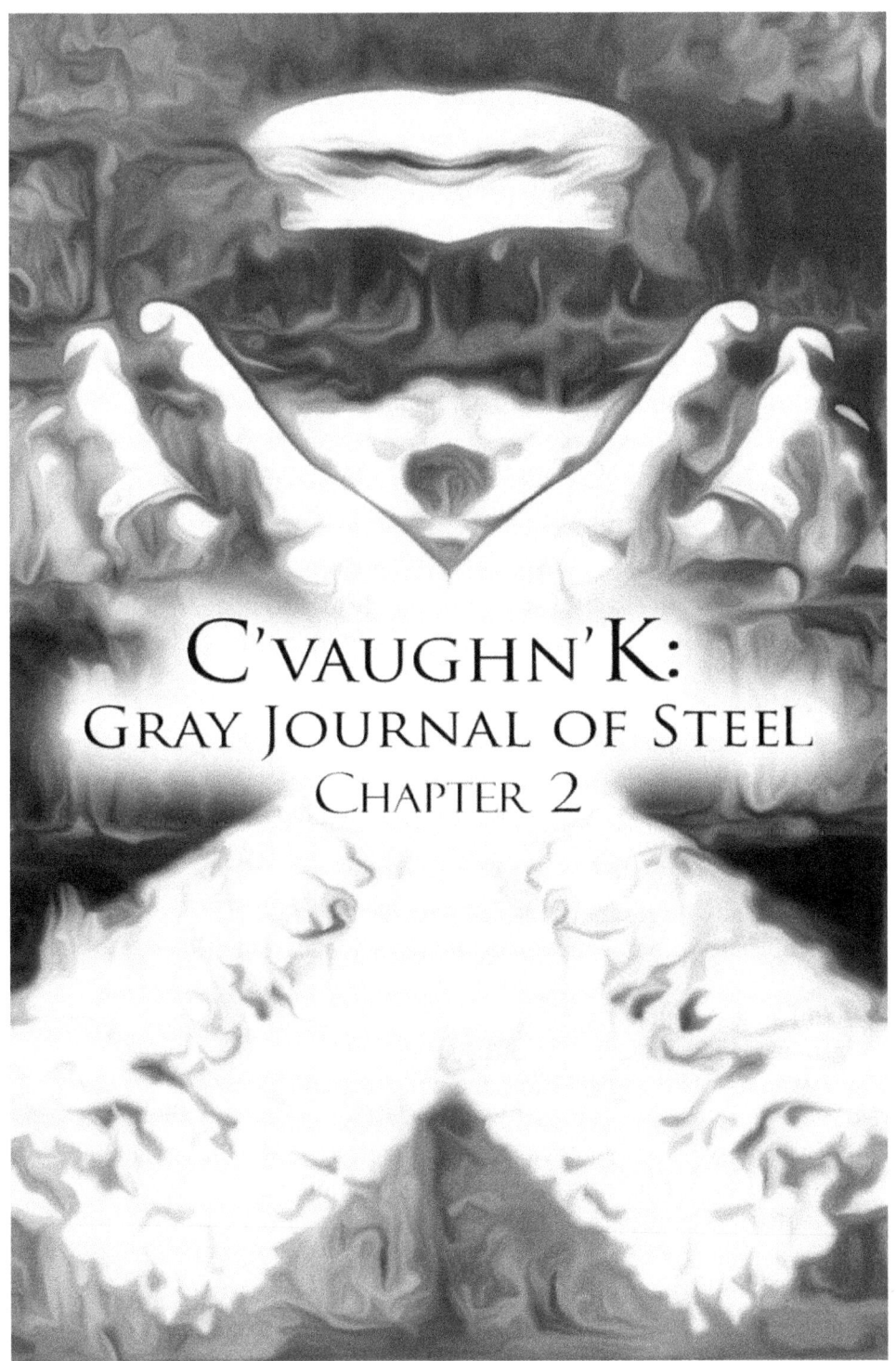

C'VAUGHN'K:
GRAY JOURNAL OF STEEL
CHAPTER 2

Story 1: **Physical Day Dreaming- Eight Palms**

Gawddess: /ˈgɑː.des/ *Infinite goddess form of a Kween aka Queen in power.*
Keenng: /kɪŋ/ *the truest form of the real King.*

Sometimes when I got writer's block.
After weeks of summoning the most complex details.

My mind often goes into an overdrive blank for hours.
With words bouncing and running from my pen.

I don't know if other writers have a special place or time.
Just to find that moment or first beginning line.

I always seem to find peace in isolated confinement.
Mostly within the corner of my basement room.

Just being down here.
My imagination always carries me into the deepest daydreams.
For which I am still unclear about the need for an enclosure.

Usually in the state of silence and lonesome.
My soul starts to talk to me like a teacher to a student.

Centering in on my emotion as I listen to my blocked heart.
Crammed with mixed storylines waiting to rip from my pineal.

Frustrated with slow pen taps against my temple.
As I debate with my energy about the topic unwritten.

So I slide my chair from the desk.
To just take a look at my blank journal.
Trying to relax my neck from the writer's arch.

Sipping my warm temp tea to break the destiny of a throat parched.
Rocking back and forth trying to feed my motive.
Mentally exhausted.

With nothing but my old inspirations for my past written
manuscripts on my mind.

It's time to think less and relax the ink before the motion.
Physical daydreaming starts to set in like an author's possession.
Pen falling to the floor as my eyes wandered wide open.

Body feeling stuck in between this and that of fiction.

Daydreaming but aware.
Of all the popular but annoying basement scats that relax me also.
Getting writer's block always puts me into a trance.
Visions are here but the mind becomes randomly absent.

Things got weird...!
I soon felt the touch of eight hands come from behind me.
Estrogen clouding the basement with darkness and damp sounds.

Pure jungle wilds in the oxygen as I inhale its feminine nature.
One body with eight caressing's... turning my desk chair.

Yet illuminating my peripheral upon seeing this deity of a
Gawddess.
Amazon features, as it seems ominous but a pleasant instance.

Melodic riffs start to play in my head smoothly.
As she dances the mating call of many frequencies in which it was
logical.

Basement surroundings are nonexistent.
As this beautiful creature moves around her ritual tattooed hands.
Never spoke or even came close to me at this point.

I assume the recognizing of this as a physical relaxer.
I have encountered many odd moments but this one seems
difficult.
Trying to inner stand her powerful dancing.

I feel swoon.
Feeling stuck to my desk throne...but sovereign.
Enduring the look of her dangerously romantic gaze.
No reason for me to speak when being lost in between.

The tones in my mind begun to fade against the drums.
Her eight palms came forth and turned me around.
She placed my pen in my hand and slowly licked my earlobe.
The deity whispered to me eight words.
(I relaxed your flesh! So write about me my Keenng.)

So I wrote without question as she left me to be.
I believe I wrote about eight palms for weeks in different ways.

I guess I was scared but moved by the deity's movements.
I hoped to see her again.
Writer's block… right…!

Sincerely, **C'vaughn'K**

Story 2: **Mental Vacation- Baggage Mind**

Just another moment of the war.
Against the work clock that seems to drag me so joyfully.

The way that it taunts my brake above my drowsy crown.
Clicking and ticking!

My patient little lunch as it awaits my core.

Dwelling through the slowest day that I trap myself into.
Yet blaming the manager's carefree attitude for it all.
Knowing that my reason was all my own, within the purpose of
needing more hours.

With only five minutes to go… BUT! DAMN IT All!
I'm starting to feel like my work shift just kicked in.
As well as, my dress shoes are finally giving.

Repetitive music on the intercom; programming us every single
day.
The hair pulling enigma of being here... is driving me mad.

I can only imagine this cash register blowing up within the minute
of my brake.
I believe my replacement has an agenda for greeting me here on
time.

Finally!
This plague of a human being slithered its way to the front.
Grinning with cigarette kite aroma drowned in its uniform.

Magazine folded under the worse armpits; you could ever fathom.
With no remorse for the time in this crap pit of a job.
(You dirty son of a bi***!)

The only thing that kept me tamed; from clawing the existence
from this prick's life.

27

Was that my thirty-minute brakes were like a drug to a waiting addict?
I needed this time to regroup and escape from the reality of my visual failures.
Walking with sleep in my stroll, and weary in my actions.

Not fully memorizing the simple lunch I gathered randomly at the job.
Which maybe was only a cold star bucks can with plain lays...
Or a dove milk chocolate.

That fact that my body allowed me.
To even make it to this dump of a crew room.

Didn't matter what it looks to me at all at this point.
I just know I can lastly start my mental vacation.

Metal chair folding and a hard round table with complete silence.
What a comfort right?

To damn sleepy to eat, but too hungry to travel mentally.
I turned the lights out and crammed a piece of chocolate in my right jaw.

Chewing it like a full course meal.
I slouched slowly in the chair, and put my hoodie over my head.

My neck resting on the back of a hard metal chair; in a cold room.
My eyelids felt like bricks, on the feet of an enemy at sea.

Embracing the darkness of my closed lids drastically.
Time began to slow down for me as I prepare for my mental vacation.

The deepness of my fatigue surpasses the complexities... of my dreams.

As I arrive in a place, where rivers are running warm across my feet.

Peculiar blue and purple skies.
Fish swim the midair, and birds fly under the oceanic.
Weird but beautiful at the same time with slight confusion as to
where I was. Across the way.

Passing the hills of raspberry flowers, and honey trees.
I can see a highway made of smooth black leather for miles.

I noticed a green bronco with a tan top, and jade tinted windows.
A mile away, but enough to notice.

That there seems to only be one person in the car.

I started to walk further towards a leather highway.
Just to reach the oncoming truck to hitch.

I can hear a slight mumble... of a very familiar song, but I can't call
it.
I finally reached the road.
I didn't have to hitchhike, because the bronco just seemed to be
stopping my way.

More like a slow cruise up in front of me as if it was sent to me
purposely.
For some reason.

I wasn't nervous by far... just curious.
As I opened the door slowly.

I can hear "Roy Ayers- everybody loves the sunshine"... at a low
volume.

I recall... that is one of my dad's favorite songs, and my own as
well.

This lucid dream just took a twist.
Dad was sitting at the wheel smoking a wood tip cherry mild.

Wool Fedora on his head, and waiting for me to get in the truck.

Granted... I'm happy to see him, but dad's been deceased for years now.
So I ignored that thought, and just drove off with my pops, and made the best of it.
He never talked much for most of the ride, but looked at me and smiled.
The proud look on his face.
He took his one hand; squeezed the top of my head, and kissed me on the forehead.

He always did show father and son love.
He then spoke lightly.

He said I love you son, and turned the music up.
I replied: I love you more dad, and then I just enjoyed the ride.

If this is a mental vacation... it was well worth it.
I hate that I have to wake up sooner or later.

Jamming with my dad is cool, Intel we see this bright a** light in front of us.

I blinked once and noticed that some idiot at work had turned the lights on.

Killed my entire vacation.
I hate this job so much, but it's time for me to get back to work.

Next time I'm locking the door because I wanted to know where dad was taking us.

Probably just cruising the open road...
Maybe next time.

Sincerely, **C'vaughn'K**

Story 3: The Elder's Essence-Smokescreen of Sorcery

Yet another scared and rising dusk.
 Glaring at my beautiful migraines hangover.

Luggage under my lashes... with red spider webs loitering in my
desert eyes.
Unrelaxed with a concrete tongue complimenting my sandy throat.

Brandy glass full of wet buds and submerging ashes spiraling.
Migraine! Excelling to my movement and giving me erotic mental
pains.

Another blackout is what I'm assuming with shaky remembrance.
Fragments of yesterday; with unstructured patterns of street lights
With a very kind homeless elder lady lurking.
I guess.

I see myself falling against a book stand, but never falling
completely.
I remember the homeless old woman holding my body up with
wisdom.

Her breath smelled like chocolate as she talked wise tales up the
way.
I see spirits between the split of her mouth... as she looks through
me as she spoke.

I felt so drained.
With weightless attempts of feeling heavy on her shoulder.

My right pants leg ripped with dry blood around the crown of my
bend.
I remember being drowsy but curious by the gorgeous elders
power.

My mind is in a twilight towards her, and my blood warming my
leg.
Migraines consumed my mental search...with odd delays.

My memories reveal a view of the elder; sitting me down against the buzzer.

How did she find my tower? ... And what happened to my damn leg?
She pulled my key from me, and I projected out of consciousness fading.

Awaking to an elevating box... with numerology taking me to the 6th floor.

I looked at the elder woman, but she was no longer an ancient beauty.

Her aura changed as the floors moved slowly against time.
From my dazed vision, she glowed like multicolor enlightenment.

What the hell is going on...? I whispered slowly.

Thinking to myself... How did she even know where I hibernated?
The 6th floor approached with sudden caution and dramatics.

I remember double looking at her; as we both came from the elevator split.
She became who she was from her elder essence.

Deep thought I was in but imprisoned to my body's weakness.
She walked me to my door and pulled another key from me.

I projected again and blacked out.
The clearer my memory got spurts of my tower room and she came across.
Mental glitch's getting better, and I see her fully.

I see a woman in her thirties glowing above my sheets.
She carries the same dolphin on her wrist as the elder did.

The look in her eyes was mercy.
She began to give my leg her lips and healed my confused wound.

Her cat eyes looked at me with gratuity in them.
She crept her claws past my wound towards the groove of my phallus.

The misunderstanding of her young transformation, and her weird seer.
I remember submitting to her force as she held me against my will.
Her vibrant erotic nurture was unknown and paralyzing to my frame.
Her tail blossomed from the back of her perfectly changed figure.

She grabbed me by the vocal cords and pinned my soul to the fabric.
Countless grinding of repetition she placed above me.

Misled and aroused by the dangers of her lioness cuts across my arms.
Her hand released my throat with tyrannical passions.

She reached between my legs for the third key, and I blacked out.
I projected again without the oversight of why.

So today is what I come to.
Another weird night as C'vaughn'K.

Sincerely, **C'vaughn'K**

Story 4: Erotic Rehabilitation- Can't Wait

Another day in the sundown city of angelic portals.

Yet trapped within its matrix of feeble ideas and romantic mischief, coexisting in one's broken forth eye.

My mind wanders the heart of my ongoing walk, of over stood pain and frustration.

Leading to its permanent pleasure and mental rehabilitation to find the inner sanctum of two minds nurturing as one tasteful fruit.

My deep meditation is indeed fulfilled with delicate channels, sensual realms, and unconquered knowledge of beyond love.

But one signal as expressed to me one soft feminine vibration of love static and flirtatious waves.

So I fall in this dream state of one individual chakra giving me access to this wifely force of passion.

Sexy as it may feel!

My spirit was like a magnet for this channel of two ultimate powers to maintain its focus, on manifesting across the astral plane of serenity.

No need for our bodies, fore we are compound as one single soul on a journey of channeling and becoming cohesive with time

Sincerely, **C'vaughn'K**

Story 5: The Traveling

This summer I decided to take a vacation to the lost islands of Hawaii's moving oceans and secret lands of historic hips.

I and some colleagues of mine were meeting are forest team out beyond the tourist away from the spinning fire with musical drums filling the sand.

This trip seems to be different than most vacations I have ever taken in my enslaved life in the estates of the loud city life I come from.

So as I prepare for my journey towards the airport, I came out the door as my two friends waited patiently for me as I slide the brakes to park.

Jenny and Richard seem to be so happy to take this trip for which it's been time long over do for this smooth flight of time spent unwisely with celebration.

I'm happy in words but yet I still feel unconfident in how I was filling about the long trip to the islands unknown.

I pass my ticket through my half-cracked window giving me a breeze down my face, as I rode towards a possible mistake that could change my life.

I step from my car as Jenny and Richard look happy and impatient but I take my cautious time when I step swiftly in my summer shoes and linen cloth of style.

Watch blinding the sun as my glass reflects my darkness at a short distance against the pupil of my prophecy to see ahead.

So our bags are carried and my car has taken refuge and we are on our way to a trip that bothers yet my spirit but we walked to the jet.

I should have shortened my introduction on behalf of only having three minutes to vanish to our luxury jet to proceed to the flight. We made it to the jet!

Bags are packed safe as Jenny and Richard rush to reach the soft seats of snakeskin interior marble frames, as white gold plush as it catches the sun.

We are seated and ready to transport ourselves to our next prior engagement but they are unaware of my prediction in emotion. I thought I needed something to make myself calm!

So I hit the button to be gifted with a bottle of red wine and a sleeping pill from an astonishing Hawaiian woman that came my way.

Her hair is golden brown like a tiger and her eyes are gray & white like an owl's wisdom, as her chest leans towards my face as she places my pill on a napkin with a red glass.

As she leaves I take my first sip as I watch her hips dance an ancient Hawaiian dance for she is designed with this groove in her walk.

As I take this pill I see that Jenny and Richard has already started passing through a dream as the jet leaves the earth.

I opened my window and closed my eyes to the sound of the jet engine putting me to sleep for hours at a time.

Silence is in the air!

Eight hours passed as we sleep strong with our comfort but the sun has come and stolen my rest as my eyes open in fatigue while seeing the islands that wait.

The jet captain speaks over the speaker and announces the landing of our timing while descending back down to the earth once more.

As we were all awake I can see three strange forest team members waiting for our arrival as the plane lands smoothly.

We prepare to reach the exit of the jet and down the stairs as they greet us with flowers around the alley of our necks while blessing us with love upon their land.

The three men are nefarious looking with the smell of jungle on their uniforms and dry blood from their knives with glasses covering their seen.

I and my colleagues walked towards the strange Caucasian men in tan rugged uniforms near the jet exit.

Jenny & Richard follow suit behind me as I can see beautiful trees lap dancing against the current of the smooth waters as coconuts feel the air.

I replied hello to the head leader out of the three guys, and he said nothing and they looked us up and down and told us… let's go to the vehicle now.

We were told to leave our bags at the jet and they will arrive at the hotel while we are out on our tour.

I and my colleagues were uncomfortable but we just carried on with things to enjoy our trip.

We begin to drive a long distance while fresh temptation carried the air as we drove through the wilderness.

Things seemed ok at first as Jenny & Richard enjoyed the ride out but I was unfocused about these three guys on this trip!

So I kept a close eye on them and enjoyed myself until we arrived at this giant creepy boat not too far from the coast.

So once again I am looking strange in the face about things I felt since we boarded the jet and landed.

Jenny & Richard ask no questions while only looking for a thrill as they walked up the boat stairs, as the sun seems to give away its spot in the sky to the moon.

The three wait for me as I am caught in deep thought but I just went ahead and grabbed my bag and came about the wooden boat.

I feel evil all around my mind but I can't give in to my human feeling and enjoy the expensive trip we have purchased.

I set in a leather chair next to the water as my colleagues enjoy the boat ride to nowhere as the sun moves closer from its position.

My compass goes crazy as the water stops moving its choppy current, and out here trees are afraid to move and the creatures of the night are vacant.

I am aware of strange things in my day but this is the oddest time of my life.

So I left my seat as my colleagues relax and drink, I confronted the captain of the ship and asked how long before we get back to land.

The captain looked me dead in my soul and replied what's the rush my friend we are here now.

His crew member screamed from the top **(LAND WHOLE)**
In my mind I think to myself I've been sitting next to that water for an hour or so and no land was found.

Once again I brushed it off and told my friends to get ready to leave the boat and we begin to all walk to the deck.

Before we left the boat the three men changed into some strange uniforms as if they were forest hunters instead of forest guides.

We paid no mind to it and walked through the island and things got weird after two hours of walking through the jungle with torches of fire.

As we walked I looked forward through the deepness of the jungle, just a mile away I can see a mountain piercing the universe.

Shaped like an endless mansion with unworkable flights of stairs for a human to even challenge.

The men seem to be in a rush to get to it as I let the three guys lead the way I stood back and whispered to my colleagues and replied that this doesn't feel right.

They told me to live a little but I was highly pissed that this was not what we had planned.

I just thought to myself I just wanted to see some different types of land and wild animals and it seems like I just arrived in the twilight.

Twenty minutes into the walk towards the mansion a huge door appeared through the gloomy night.

The three of them opened the door, and as we went forward the door closed rapidly as the floor falls miles and miles underground.

I feel like my ankle is broken but it's just sore with a great amount of dust feeling the oxygen.

I yelled out (Jenny) (Richard) they answered short of breath both saying we are ok just startled as all, what about you Adonis?

I said I'm fine but where the hell is the guide team?

We have not heard them or seen them since we fell down this weird hole of dust and dirt.

As things got stranger I started to think harder in my mind. Jenny said to me with nervousness, *it smells dead down here*.

I replied to Jenny.
Let's just look for them.

After thirty minutes of searching, we heard the noise of loud grinding rocks nearby assuming it was them.

We came to a stop in front of two doors leading to this weird room full of stone pillars.

We walked slowly as we saw one of the men go underground through a small wooden door but something was different about them.

Their voice was different like the grunting of beast while hearing other aggressive vibrations under the ground.

So I just didn't care after that, I told Jenny to put her foot over the door so I can lock it because we were all afraid.

But the demonic man bust through the floor throwing Jenny to the wall as Richard is nowhere to be found.

We ran through the darkness as the fire goes out, and I am looking for Jenny through the glare of the fire dyeing.

I finally reach her hands and we ran for our lives feeling around for a place to hide, until the morning sun so we can escape the demonic men screaming through the night for our essence.

We found a stone door and fell asleep exhausted from everything that was happening and the screams seem to have stopped for a reason.

As we slept, me and Jenny feeling confused and afraid of the short encounter.

The stone door begins to move and pull the hinges from the rock, and I and Jenny woke with fear, and when the door moved there was so much light.

Five Hawaiian ancient-looking men's hands reach through the light but I couldn't defend us for we are weak.

They helped us from the hole after we blacked out again and we woke up on a boat of roses and Hawaiian people surrounding us.

As we rode the boat down the lake I saw far up in the forest tree the three men impaled to large sticks with symbolic writing written on their flesh.

The people of the land took the demonic men and made an example of them, as the boat floated across the water passing their grave in the sky.

They took me and Jenny to a hill and we saw Richard tide up on the ground in one of the secret tents containing his possession.

It took ten men to drag him to a bed of sand to take the demon from him.

His eyes were amber and black and his neck looks broken, and his skin looks like veins busting with muscles of a gladiator with hellish roaring teeth.

They fixed him faster than the twist of cold wind and ever since then… all I can think about is the traveling.

Sincerely, **C'vaughn'K**

Story 6: The Serenaders Lounge

I guess it's another brewing night of open bottles of exotic wine and promises of less liquor crying from my old wooden nightstand.

As my temptation spills from my staggering lush against the wood grain approaching the springing cot of my discomfort.

My eyes see nothing but the wind as it blows through my window sweeping the sweat off my forehead, and down my face as my head free-falls into the center of my pillow.

Mind-wandering as my hand reaches into my pants for my gold lighter yet gazing into the reflection of its metal looking for my flame… repeating once **(baby I am all burnt out).**

A single tear escapes freely from my left eye as I reach for my last cigarette in a crushed box attempting to quit with a craving to smoke the pain away.

The moon glares in through the thin texture of my curtains yet sashaying over me dancing with the wind! As the sounds of night breaks-in through my half-opened window.

I am thinking to myself what am I doing here?

The tiles on my floor are rising to paradise, as well as the sealing paint is falling into ruins! Everything seems to be damaged and coping with the verdict of my whole life.

As my cigarette burns, and ashes stain my sheets as I forget it is held in my hand without the flicking of its time lit and put to my lips wondering for hours on this cot.

The room begins to rotate in my drunken rage and the alcohol is playing tracks in my mind. I am seeing shadows of laughter pulling at my soul and tempting me to waste away.

But a strong whisper cuts through the ignorance of loud hyenas in my mind and it yelled *(Boy Pull Your Self Together)* I said to myself who is that?

The whisper replied again *(Boy Pull Your Self Together!*
So I opened my dead eyes and forced my drunken weight to rise against the fabric of a future hangover and the whisper replied again.)

(You need to breathe once more… so you need to get dressed and Leave)

I drop my left leg against the left side of the bed as my right leg followed sluggishly behind. With my back and head humped over my shoes.
I sighed deeply!

Intentionally to embrace the relief of screaming walls of seldom pain in my dark depressing apartment.

I stood firmly while not being aware that my legs are like ice melting under the sun next to an ending edge of the mountain.

So I brace my stand and slowly dragged myself to the bathroom to wash my face, and awake the man I once was before the liquor took me hostage.

As the water fills the sink!

I can hear the skipping of my heart hesitating to take the next drum note as the liquor on my breath is burning the trim of my lips, and coating my throat.

I refuse to look in the mirror and gaze upon the stubborn facial expression that I give off.
But I cannot escape it.

As I kneel into the face bowl of water to cleanse the aura of my mind, to just reach some state of focus.

I can see the sober side of me as I come from the water, and I slightly grabbed a towel from the broken rack in the bathroom and dried my face.

I turn towards the bathroom door and begun to leave rapidly half sober against my wobbling legs and dizzy vision.

I opened the door, took a halt, and had to figure out where am I about to go to get the feeling of breathing again.

So I just left and thought about just winging it for once instead of planning the worst place to release.

So as I walked the hall of my apartment building my thoughts is like fire in a burning house!

If it can't get out, it will burn right through my imagination.
So I just needed to find some source of thrill.

But where would I find a thrill in the city that never sleeps?
So I finally arrive on the outside staggering and trying to walk a straight line.

So I said to myself the night is warm… with streets crowded with motion like roaches with jobs, but I bear with how I am feeling and I just walked the distance.

I was walking by an alley that I walked by all the time coming from the bar that held me captive after late hours of work.

But as I walked! I felt different than my regular depressed and drunken days with an ashtray on my tongue and red eyes gazing through silver smoke from the alley sewer.

So as I got to the end of my apartment building.
I see two gold stone pillars, and a ladder going nowhere.

Yet glowing from the far end of the alley right from the corner of my eye.

I was afraid to look directly towards it but I stood stiff as time within myself, only to embrace my new level of a natural high. Sincerely, **C'vaughn'K**

Story 7: **Green Budded Feelings-Bench Rolling**

Today boredom was fluctuating its brutal task to keep me captive & seated.

With every slithering intention to keep me pondering my next agenda.

Why is it that my fingertips fell so tingly and agitated?

Unsure as I sit upon this splintering park bench.

Which seems to be intriguing my fatigued recess.

Lighting my goals, and just fading away with a bus ticket to nothing.

I guess all stories are not meant to be long when you've mastered the trip, with my eyes on a slit while my sight performs me a show of numbness towards the feeling of rolling once… but forever more.

Sincerely, **C'vaughn'K**

Story 8: **Hot Brewing Tea- Yawning**

A midnight walk to the kitchen with half-sleep muscles still at rest.

Z's captive in my pupil's corners followed with the shift sounds of wood boards.

Arriving at a cold stove waiting to do my bidding within the turn of a slow boil.

A copper jail of alkaline to simmer and brew above an adamant fire.

I know it's late but worth the wait for hot herbs submerged in sizzling water.

That ginger steam with cane sugar and a slight drip of fresh night honey.

It soothes my cotton mouth that's just waiting on this shiny gold pot to scream at me.

Leaning against the island.
Arms crossed.
Wandering eyes.

Just thinking to myself.
How many sliced lemons would balance the end?

Stuck in my pondering about the perfect hot tea.

Brewing thee insomnia to aid my yawning nights of ceiling staring.

The tea finally screams and breaks my concentration of standing dreams.

Such a beautiful noise.

It's time to prepare my cure for dark staring in the pitch black.

I can smell the ginger as I get close to retrieving the long patient taste.

Yielding to the beginning of the most perfect tea ritual.

Fresh ginger & herbs, lemons, honey, and cane sugar with light cinnamon at bay.

As the flame dies so rapidly I allowed the tea seven minutes to be.

I see a half-moon relaxing as I grab my favorite teacup & wooden spoon.

With all the ingredients prepared patiently.

Pouring the hot ginger tea upon the rim slowly to let the oxygen caress it.

As the tea falls from the copper release.

I can taste the brewing mix with perfection as the liquid settles.

With toast on my mind and jam on my thoughts.

My actions are deeper than hot brewing tea and unable to rest.

Furthermore, I take my tea and toast to the upstairs balcony in the bedroom.

Quiet wind with uncluttered skies and southern stars.

At peace as I take a bite and sipped the herbals hot glaze.

It's a laze night to fall asleep under the sky in my old chair

Tea just cools, as the steam runs from every breeze.

Sincerely, **C'vaughn'K**

Story 9: **Roses Hurt So Good**

I woke up confused this sunrise, in a dripping alley next to her dying roses and pigeons over my eyelids.

Blood painted in a splash across my ripped shirt without wounds of my own but I appear to feel deception.

I try to lift my anchored down body but I trembled, boiling my soul in a warm alley puddle.

What has happened to me, why am I punished for the fact of gifts and celebration?

I lay here with roses of bondage with its nectar dripping without any water but dyeing.

My anchored hand lifts from the greasy alley water to catch rain from the crying cloud.

Roses, I shall give you more life but can't promise that your petals won't fall for we both are damaged.

The sound of the screaming streets keeps me awake and aware of my inner pain.

Dark Images flare in my brain trying to rekindle its fatal position. The thorn of the roses is cutting my palm but it hurts nearly to its appointed duty.

I try again to rise but the moon intercepts my sun dial, what is happening to me?

So my left hand tries to grab the rusted can, as my back drag the wall of flesh… my torture is misled.

As I turn around to the brick wall catching my balance with a fuzzy memory.

Lightning strikes the crying cloud as if it were a battered child threatened for wanting attention.

As the storm pursue flashing images of two dark beings touching me like queen cobras on a lion; but I fought.

Flashes of me screaming stop, for I was drugged by these dark female entities molesting my spirit.

Thought of me dragged out of a hot tub, and forcefully aroused by their wicked nature.

Ancestors help me, why are these thoughts of me grazed so deeply by these things?

Flashes of a horn headed woman swallowing my lap, and the second bat-winged woman's nails engraving spells inside my chest.

The cloud has stopped crying but one last tear saves my life, as I look up to see rose petals falling slowly.

This righteous single tear comes from the high gates of thus unknown to wonder.

The cloud gives me its last remorse, and falls in my eye and cries out through me to have peace.

I don't know why I am here, in this alley with no garden to pick this bundle of fine roses.

As this tear works through me like the venom of a snake, but yet from a pleasant cloud.

Even thus I am saved finally somehow; ancestors forgive me if at the time the thorns of the roses hurt so good…

Sincerely, **C'vaughn'K**

Story 10: **Smoky Legs in Blue**

One midnight I was bored out of my senses and decided to take a smooth jazzy walk down to The Serenaders Lounge.

It's a classy hole in the joint that gives off a strong smell of short conversations, lingering cigars, and clashing beer mugs.

So I wore my favorite black suit.
With marble buttons and my tie lusting my neck frame.

As I prepared my royal fit, I leave from the condo… dragging my fragrance from the room to a lobby of magazine flips and suede chairs.

I lead forward as my dress shoes pushed the ground caressing the pavement as leaves crunch under my stride.

My move is like chess with too many pawns, and I as one emperor taking my move to midnight.

As the walk bared short of its distant miles lusting to find incitement once more.

I finally arrive at The Serenaders Lounge alone and ready to contemplate my boredom.

It's dark and crowded with lights that are smoky with residue feeling the air with moans and flirt.

I walk slowly to my favorite table in the corner, right by the stage in the shadow of security and relaxation.

I await the attractive but older flavor with tress and patient for a bottle of Pama Pomegranate with a lemon-lime hugging the glass of my ice.

Neo-soul jazz is sophisticating the air with a smooth sexy grab on my ears.
You know that feeling you get when something beautiful is writing a novel of you in their eyes.

The ambiance is drowned with her tapping heel, bass playing the rugged wood floor to the bass guitar pick.

So I decided to take a look across the two stages… towards her corner shadow; is she an imagination or a real difference?

I can barely recognize her through the smoke, or the shape of her beauty in the dark corner.

All I can see is the cigarette smoke, the eyes, and the glittering jiggle of her sparkle when the black light hits them softly, as she adjusts her seating.

Damn tonight feels odd because I and this glorious strange woman were the only ones left in The Serenaders Lounge.

So I take my drink to sit with her, but when I set upon the loose chairs no one was there just me, and what I thought were smokey legs in blue.

Left with only two shots of what the hell is happening.

Sincerely, **C'vaughn'K**

11680

#679

#678

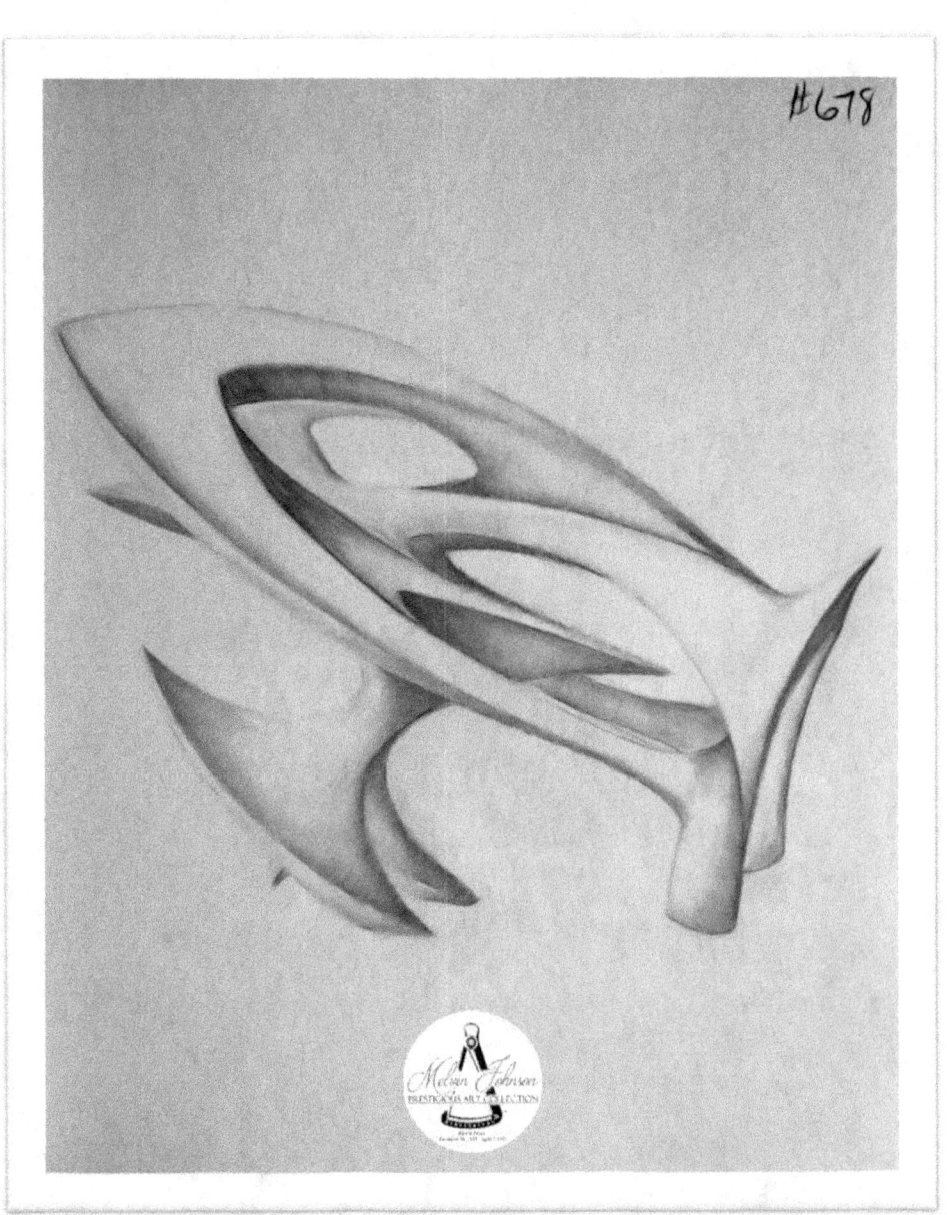

Poetry, Spoken Word, and Quotes
Chapter 3

A Divine Master
(Quote)

"Sometimes I don't bother… to look in the mirror in the wake, fore it does not have to repeat what I already know what I am… a divine master."

~B.GKL

A Petty Fight with My Soul

Man, I went to sleep last night…And last night sleeping.
I went to sleep last night… And my dreams started creeping.
A shadow walked up to me & said *(WHAT THE HELL ARE*
YOU DOING HERE)....!

I spoke to myself out loud, why the hell are you in my mind?
The shadow once again said.

(WHAT THE HELL ARE YOU DOING HERE)...!
I repeated it twice at a time... and it said
(MAN I AM YOUR SOUL, AND I'M KIND OF FED UP WITH
YOUR WIT)….!

What are you doing with the bags?
Are you trying to leave real quick?
I say hey soul I can't just let you go.

(I AM LIKE WATER YOU GOT TO LET FLOW).

Look at this world we get the stroll together.

(I CAN FIND SOMEONE ELSE TO TREAT ME BETTER).

You're my soul.
You have been here since I was born.

(LOOK AT THE PERSON YOU'VE BECOME…
LOOK AT THE PATH THAT YOU HAVE FORMED)

Soul, I'm not the one that made the rain.
I'm not the one that made the storm.

My soul keeps arguing with me.
Telling me what it's going to do.
I yelled to my soul:
(SIT DOWN, AND LET ME TALK TO YOU!)
I got a couple of minutes.

Life is getting short.
From a couple!
To a few!

My soul replied:
(HAY, LOWER YOUR TONE, AND LOWER YOUR VOICE.
BECAUSE I DON'T HAVE TO STAY HERE!
EVERYTHING IS ON FIRE, AND I BELIEVE I SEE NO
OTHER CHOICE.)

Hey soul.
I know we've been through a lot together.
You've seen me make the wrong decisions.

(DAMN THAT MAN…
EVERY TIME I TRY TO GIVE YOU THE RIGHT
THOUGHT… OR THE RIGHT CONSCIOUS, YOU KEEP
FORCING US IN THE WRONG CONDITIONS).

Hey soul…Chill out…! Your bass is too high.

(WELL I CAN'T TELL… I THOUGHT WE WERE MAN.
YOU DON'T HAVE ANOTHER ALIBI).

Don't even sit here and nag.
Because this is wrong!
You are trying to abandon me.
Leaving me with an empty shell or maybe a toe tag…!

I am the car…You're the driver.
My soul looked me in my eyes…& replied.

(FORGET THAT.
YOU ARE NOTHING BUT A BAG OF MEAT.
I AM THE SURVIVOR.
YOU USE TO SMOKE…YOU USE TO GANGBANG.
YOU USED TO SAY ANYTHING TO MAKE YOURSELF
FEEL BETTER.

WHILE GETTING US BOTH CAUGHT UP IN WILD THINGS…!
ALSO FULFILLING THE NEED OF YOUR LUST!
ALL YOU CARED ABOUT BACK IN THE DAY.
IS WHAT YOU CAN TOUCH.

I WANTED LOVE FROM ONE WOMAN.
ALL YOU DESIRED WAS A CRUSH.

I TRIED TO GIVE YOU A WIFE.
INSTEAD, YOU WANTED A PROMISCUOUS LIFE.

I AM GOING TO TELL YOU HOW TO MOVE FORWARD.
WE CAN MANIFEST TOGETHER.
ONLY IF YOU SIT DOWN, AND LISTEN.)

I can't believe my soul.
Is telling me what it's going to do, and how things are going to roll.
My soul set back and draw forward.
We squared up and was ready to go.

My soul is going to attempt to fight me.

We've had each other's back forever.
From playpens to play dough!
.
From bad food…To spiritual rules!
From nights!
From monsters in the closet!
To hearing creepy sounds dripping from the faucet.

We've been afraid together.

All I needed you to know.
Was that I would appreciate it if you stayed!
My soul replied:
(DAMN THAT… TIME IS UP)

My soul looked at the time.
Then all I can feel is my pride fading down.
My soul replied:
(BEFORE I LEAVE)
(GIVE ME YOUR MIND… YOU DON'T DESERVE THAT
CROWN)
SINCE YOU CAN'T APPRECIATE THE LOVE THAT I
BRING FOR US
THROUGH YOU…!
I AM GOING TO TAKE WHAT I GAVE, AND SHOW YOU
WHAT I MEAN TO DO.

I WILL GIVE YOU ONE MORE DAY.
TO PROSPER BEYOND THE HUMAN FLAW!
I NEED YOU TO INHALE…EXHALE, AND RELEASE!

I turned around.
As the fire of the beast…!
Spewed outside of my mouth!
My body reminds me of a car.
More than likely an undefined house!
It's so dysfunctional.
Nothing works properly.
My gears are rotating & moving.
There's nothing here stopping me.
My soul is still lingering to leave.
Leading me to bleed…!

So I replied Again:
Soul!

Sit here, and help my mind receive.

The notion to get to know you… Please.
Stay here within me.
Soul…I love us as we.

I feel incomplete.
My soul shook hands…!

61

Willing to give it another chance!
Towards guiding my path.

~B.GKL

A Soul

My soul.

Is like paradise for which I am not open.

To any oblivion choice of pain involved.

I am the leaves that fall.
Where there are no trees at all.

I am immortal without dreams to breathe or exist.

I am wealthy without the desire to be humanly rich.

I am forever before there was.
A soul.

~B.GKL

Adjust

I adjust.
Until my eyes can see.

I tried to be.
What the world could free.

Will no human die for you as well as die for me?
So I adjust to the wisdom I try to speak.

Cursive words I consume thus eat.
Leading a life with its herbs in soft heat.

Let my hands be.
My fingers feel broke.

My palm slowly reaching towards a thin rope!
With three unreal wishes to never assume death!

Depressed to what serenity as but can never have.
Bathe to stay pure with a filthy life.
Only that in which we feel we cannot save.

With serious temptation!
Mental migration!
My pillow in tears relation!

Creation of disbelief in what my taste buds may be tasting.
Face off to the world but facing.
The true thought is that I will always obtain abrasion.

Having sand in my eyes and blinking dust.
Misguided single rush.
If there is no love refueling my passion with lust.
Speaking out loud in quiet surroundings that hush.

With one knife taunting the swift binding of my wrist.
Split! With fist! With thrush!

Cheeks red scared straight without her smiles blush.
Sleep in my eyes.
Vision scared to sleep.
I must.
Adapt to the sun.
On bright nights as I await until… my pupils
Adjust.

~B.GKL

Back Of My Voice
Keenng- The truest form of the real King.

How did it feel?
When I came outside to feel the wind breeze!

You don't give a damn.
When you lay down in your bed & your bones start to inhale.
Trying but can't breathe.

Trying to focus on which path to take when I leave the driveway!
How can I open my eyes this day & gain a different smile?
Deciding on which way my hands are going to lie!

I feel like every time I put my hands in my pocket.
I'm pulling out the cushion of lint.

Thinking about all the paths & things…!
That I have done.
Towards all the money that I have spent…!

Trying to remember all the pain that I may have caused!
Among most places that I have gone.

I am a gentleman by the soul.
A Keenng to the strong & the weak with no offense!
I'm tired of being known for.
Waking up in the sunshine with fire like dragons.

You never see & know that I was created in flames.
Eating the fire every day as one's passion.
Give me something from the inside of me & call it a nation.
Every time I wake up I think that I am deceased.
I wake up alive & different to a brand new revelation.

Patients…!

Gather me.
Like you would gather leaves in between the lines of a rake.

You don't know where I am at.
You can't see that I am part of the earth.
Something that you can never forsake!

My body is here.
But my soul has never entered the element of this time.
It doesn't even matter.
I am a king always.
No matter if I lost gold, platinum to dimes.

I embrace sun gazing.
It makes me get this vitamin inside my soul.
To make my insides strong…!

My bones are not brittle anymore.
I feel stronger than yesterday.
I don't have time to play chess or checkers.
Neither the board games of life that you play.

My sequence is different.
Just like it was before I went to sleep

I sat down & drunk this water…Allowing it to run down deep.
I take a deep gasp.
All I see are lights & chem-trails inside of the sky.
You won't kill me… You can destroy my body… Or torture me
off.

You can take the back of my voice.
Within my being...!

~B.GKL

Beach Of Brown Sand

Release the carbon sand.
From her current swing under the moon's stride.

Float through my scalp.
Tingle through my follicles.
For I'm at your flowing mercy.

Naked wind bounces against your wide body of sea.
Holding its mysteries of the most needed.

My mouth is dry but your existence is pure hydration.
Consistent as a waterfall.
Close as thee unknown beneath a drifting boat.

For the glare of your moon yields me.
In a circling echo.
Above the different and the misunderstood.
I can't help to drift and be pulled.
Into your open surroundings.

Your soft bed of brown sand at my reach.
Take me away.
My beach of brown sand.

For me and you shall manifest.
Our haven of sand and comfort.
Be my beautiful distance.
Of beautiful brown sand.

~B.GKL

Beautiful Feelings

Sista- Melanin ebony soul being considered a sister in depth.

Stories trapped behind the ambiance of your masquerading gaze,
without tyrannical weather.
Feelings, being ignored by the rapid flash crafting thee Hennessey
brown in your study retinas.

Statue, and placed with frozen lips, speaking inside the forward
statement... of modeled hunger.
Channeling, the soft candy skin you convey; unveil the celestial
Sista.

~B.GKL

Between Her Awake

Awake.
Over twisted sheets.

The body's submerged within last night.
Tight hold against the gentle.

A slow glance to my left.

To admire her aura squeezing the patient time.

Seek my dark lucid travels.

Her mental moaning clouding the room's tension.

Sexy mentions.
Fading in this cogitation.

Lovemaking.
Between her awake

~B.GKL

Body of Bad Dreams

Plenty of love has passed this heart, as well as hate, has stood
before my arrogant presence.

Being humble is a reward, towards stubborn hand holing pride to
protect a flawed legacy.

Forced to put out fires with your tears, while you, yourself are
engulfed in flames.

How can I put out anything as a man born from gasoline?

Sleep deprivation setting in, as my eyes require pure rest in the
darkness of blinks.

Placing my arms around my ribs, and brake my neck to the sky
while seeing discomfort.

Body of power, but fatal to lose what I eat from the sun.

All thought without a clear head is a body of bad dreams.

Run its chorus, and seek nothing but hollow tones.

For I am the way of a healing mind.

~B.GKL

Body to Mind, Give Her the Glamour
Yoni- *The essence of women's universal life-giver and love*

Sometimes!
Love can take you to dark places.
That is sometimes good.

You have to appeal to a woman's intellect.
Just From becoming different.

Give her the sensation of glamour.
Truly loving the body & mind of vibrating the soul!

All I can see.
Is that I can't wait to get to the room.
I can't wait.
To grab her legs!
To show you the deepest part of my meditation.
There was no need to hesitate or have any patience.

So let's rush or do nothing at all.
I have already made love to you in my mind.
I have not even made it to the house.

I was focused on you before I even arrived.
I see us in the back of a car.
Slowly ripping open the seats!

Let the cotton springs jump and making her heartbeat.

Everything that you have going on.
I need going on, on me.

The only thing that I wish to focus upon.
Is all that I see.

Let me brace your yoni.
Twist you.
Keeping you upon thee.

You crushed my body.
You crushed my spine.
Motivating every part of me…

You don't think I know how you feel.
I knew before I came.
That you tried to conjure me!

Lighting candles of sage around you.
Surrounding yourself with love chants!
She Provokes love possessions of my sexuality.

I am trying to give you what I am.
I'm trying to lie upon it.
I will walk through mud to get that grub.

Let me slay you and push you to the highest plane.
Let's go to places where people are afraid to grow.

I'm trying to send you there.
Bring the stars to me.
So I can bring you the moon and show you that it's hard to see.

I am trying to give you the feel of the wilderness.
I am trying to reveal to you that you are mother earth.
Within my sexual tendencies!
I want to growl. I want to hiss.
I want to love it.
I want to rub you down with the brown hand of my fist.
Upon your curves, I love it so much.
Fade into my gravitational pull.

Are you addicted?
I'm conflicted!
With your mind!
Yet the beautiful ways that you are gifted.

I bring about the legs of her yoni.
I want to break it down…

If you were a drug!
I would take you.
Sniff you, break you, and love you.

Forefeeling your desires.
Of what I need and what you want.

I will take you on top of this bedsheet.
Rip down your fabrications and drive it in deep.
I have something for you.
That organization.

That she tries to organize.
Take my surprise on this plane that we are on.
Your legs!
Your knees!
Please...
Give me what I conquer.
I shall be your lion.
Come to my arms.

Body to mind, Give her the glamour.

~B.GKL

Born As a Rock
Kween- The truest form of the real queen.

Some people believe.
That rocks don't bleed.
That's just because I am holding my weight.
In this one spot.

With moss growing & grass willing to receive.
Stress held in.
Not being able to move.

Created inside a jungle.
Only to be permanently set in a circular groove.
To shape out the structure of the rock of my body.
Wind the blowing across my surroundings.

Grounding my passion.
To one day.
Make that greater move.

I'm trying not to think too deep.
Or in-depth.
To everything that walks across my path.
All I can do is just watch.
The many things that crawl or intercept.
Gathering my thoughts about not being a rock or stone.

Although at one point.
It becomes so profound.
To continue being here alone.

Being strong is not what I give up.
Because you can never break me.
Being strong is the motive that I possess.
In which I could only be myself.

My vision is narrow.
Thinking beyond this muddy sunken spot.

People in this world can't comprehend.
The life of a rock.
Us being the elements that we are created to be.
Being handed the wrong things outside of the wound.

We come to this world.
Becoming things that we are not aware of.
Avoiding greater obstacles in nature.

Weeds of distance.
Needs you to be what it pursues.
I overstand this from a high hill.
That everything is colorful & mostly green.

On the count of my position.
Of where my rock is presently placed.
All I can see.
Is fatal dreams.

Beams.
Stopping me from hurdling over to the next goal.
Sometimes.
I get tired of walking forward.
Some days I might just want to roll.

Up or down the steep.
That's the thrill in my life.
Born as a rock in the position.
That I am in.

So I do things for a reason.
No matter how much everything changes around me.
I am a rock.
Every got damn season.

Please understand me.
You have to look at my abstract.
No matter how many ways you look around me.
I am.

76

My best front & back.
I feel like.
What I look like.
In front of your eyes.
You see me & assume nothing but aggression.
An animal if I may say.
When you are born as such.
As what I am.
To be only a rock.

You don't pick what you want on that day.
You are what you are.

If you are human.
At heart.
You are born to be a warrior of meaning.
No matter if it's summer.
Winter.
Or got damn it spring.

My passion is to be.
The best that I can see.
Myself becoming which is better.

People don't understand that even rocks grow soft.
In times of pain.

As long as moisture runs across it.
From the lake above the head.
It may seem strange.

That rock moves an inch every day.
Hoping to yet move.
Desiring to blow like leaves out in the random.
In time.
As a stone that I am.
Born to be a child into an adult.
Adult to becoming royalty.
Royalty manifesting into an infinite being.

I will watch myself create my passion.
From a rock.
To a got damn mountain.
I will not be moved.

In my mindset.
To be the rock that I am.
I am hoping to become a mountain.
Only to be a planet.
You can become something so great.
That you can become nothing at all.
To be the greatest energy
Outside of yourself.
Is to become power.
Yet this is just the life of a rock.

I remember being a pebble.
I moved. I merged.
I shift from the ground.
As the layers starting to slide.
You can hear me by the sound.
Earthquakes that I make.
Only when I am tempted.

At the same time.
When you pass by my solitary.
You may hurt yourself.
If you would just relax.
My **Kween**.
Just take a seat upon my crown.
You would never get hurt.
My only expectations of you.
Is to look at me more then.
Just being born as a rock.

~B.GKL

Broken Chess Pieces- The Reality Game

Shattered billy clubs broke across the screams of my warrior call to just breathe, with knees glued to my neck and life fading upon concrete leaves.

Thieves smirk and cuff my bent limbs while channeling their greatest hatred for my strength and royal brown skin tint.

Pent against the world's frustration, while cameras recorded but never risk their lives; but rather watch and outcry in fear behind a digital device.

Soul advice whispering in my mind that this pain is temporary and life is short-ranged; momentary exchange of melanin essence, forced towards its higher self.

Wealth is within, as the body may be considered a prison or home, with people trying to violate the wellbeing of yourself with their washed brains for greedy power.

Cowards writing themselves into the history of others, while feeding their lust for the true demise of another with different tones but similar organs.

Origins of bloody stories written in buckshot fire and chased, while getting some cardio with grass wiping the sweat from my jogging face.

A taste of immense karma is in place, for all the death given in the standards of people who are blind to their destruction in this reality.

They rather be a cavity in this realm and continuing the abuse of our women by shaming them in the streets with touchy hands and aggressive slams to the ground.

Sounds of racist screams and van door tires snatching the young and naive from playgrounds, with no trace of evidence; but a family of tears left behind.

All lines being crossed and nothing is purely done, as most cast News that provides cover to protect the foolish lies they need us to believe.

Like the trees that are dying near towers of five that feed hate into the beauty of nature, while greenbacks are falling into the pockets of silent investors… with the identity of unworked hands.

The chance of having a choice is being taken, as murder becomes advanced but ever so patient.

Placement of chess pieces and pawns has been forced in the millions, while some squeeze through the cracks to fight for the people and then collapse.

Liberal hacks that betray their own for just a plate of pie… at the table of vultures just waiting to devour you with wine.

Mines of bloody unjust stories, but now is the moment to end all riots of fire, just to fulfill the natural virtue of universal justice… while standing as one remedy.

The penalty of all things pursued by past plains of diabolical sweet dreams to eat the minds of our being as people of mysterious feet.

Seek no worry of revenge, for the times, will soon provide the sword into the heart of the card player that deals any deck in this rigged game.

Change is a calm word used to make the mind docile, and enabling our anger and heartfelt passions to destroy the things that put this planet down.

Remember that a masked clown is a nonentity, without a ruler to command it to be a bigger fool, or forcing it to hide its ugly ways with pounds of fake smiling foundation.

Application of cosmetic veils hiding their true intent to kill us with what they feel we don't see in blind daylight.

We fight to see with dirt kicked in our eyes, and try to walk with our peace held high, while the rules of this toxic land are commencing plains to take us out.

Shouts and screams and political guillotines, handing dead headed green; too many palms with means to cause the problem and be the solution in one between.

Streams of bodies under a flag of misled, with strips of racial conditions; written in debt and television, tell a vision of lies to the kingdom of our minds.

Time showing us repeated times of history being a game reality... the pieces of chess broken and pushing us off the board, in which we gave construction under torture.

Enforcers of depopulation and hate for anything growing and holding its weight or even having thoughts of controlling the fate of our own.

Gone in a blink, and turned into balloons, bears, melted candles, and libation drinks; teary face songs with no justice but the remembrance of tear gas caressing my lungs.

Death comes and everyone's violin strums, and then the deceased becomes a social media urn, digital ashes with no justice with video evidence and shotgun.

Father and son pledging their privilege, and try to weasel while edging towards innocent, as one great soul has lost his life for running with clean hands.

Another stands in pain, as the militant melanin woman is beat and killed; for having the strength to deal with the bad side of enforcement to conceal her power.

Our real stories shall never be forgotten, as the chess game will soon be recreated by the real checkmate… with us uniting the plate of all love and strength.

~B.GKL

Brown Flower

Kween- The truest form of the real queen.
Keenng- The truest form of the real King.

As the sky is blue her petals are brown.
The evolution of a garden Kween has evolved from the damp
muddy ground.

Blow my brown flower.
With rain showers and convey that sweet sound.

Of her roots twisting and turning leaves.
Sticks with mud to compose the earthly Keenng's crown.

Brown flower drops her petals.
Remove them slowly as if it was an elegant silk gown.

My tree is like the pleasure sliding deep where raindrops drown.

Dampish and erotic.
Brown rain forest amid her inner nectar.
Can I keep you confined in my flower pot?
Rubbing your soft texture.

Her flower grows and flows like a runaway cloud.
Gone like a free feather.

Her stems are wide and her body takes motion.
Like the blowing of rugged weather.

Her flower is prudent, sexy, and sturdy.
Coated with thorns with no pressure.

Can my bed be your garden of eternal pleasure?

Brown flower I like when you amend your clothes.
To look like a different rose.

Can I be the earth?

Gripping the roots of your toes.
When you sprout.
It's like a detonation.
Between your blossoming honey grove.

My eyes are the sun that keeps the pose.
Of your unique abstract.
That makes you a brown rose.

~B.GKL

Canvas Pleasure

Brush against my affections and paint a canvas of my desires.

Feuding with your heart to mend, to create the perfect stroke of genius.

Imagine my love for many purposes of art.

Colors of many emotions splashed against the blank square of artistry.

I am your painter!

Am I not?

~B.GKL

Chainless Immunity: The Black Key

My benign melanin blood… shall hold power among the burden of
my skin tones fury.
The jury of my Immersed painful waters, with combative tears
uncaptured but confined.
Remind my flesh of what rational motives can change my present
scars, from my historic recollection.

Disaffection from all fragile ghettos and suburbs… while
becoming the middle throne influence of being the scale.
Wholesale ambitions… are sold to the chainless minds of our
youth without any immunity against illusions of false change.

Deranged ideas are created to remove the black key, from the glow
of light holding thought from the frontal lobe.
The wardrobe of energy ignites the infernal blaze of confidence to
make it through another day without social conflict.

Convict like closure with claustrophobic hopes, while feeling life
without the release of having freedom anxiety.
Irony sleeps at the bloodline of my heart's front door, by kin I
assume is family; but makes me feel like an intruder.

Abusers of words, many are without reason… of interpreting the
chainless conditions of my true liberation and roots.
Institute of my groundwork, shall be honored with civility towards
the love of my sovereign observation.

The gyration of spiraling dear ones slaughtered, while the past
times of my revenge lead the chronicles of their omnipresence.
Pheasant flock of agents, trying to rebuild the links of ligament
bondage and now hunted like boar for bait.

Negate the effects of all misled by a delusion of deceit, covered in
the sweet candy of desire and forged expectation.
Isolation is now my true peace to maintain, with the allowance of
my choice of what I care for from within.

Pen of ink… please release the black keys of my chainless immunity, fore my eyes are only a chained reminder of others lost.

~B.GKL

Chocolate Water 1

Allow, your candle like kisses to liquefy, upon my melanin recline.

Embrace our relaxing natures… unlead, random and lingering minds.

You desire my raspy speech, and I long for your pure vocal fruit.

Be my hummingbird; silence the garden that makes the world mute.

You are the only…!

~B.GKL

Chocolate Water 2

Yoni-Verse: / yoh-nee:vurs/ *the essence of women's universal life-giver and love, perceived as more in-depth creating energies.*

Allow her delicious voice, to dissolve upon the dark tower of my mushroom.

Consume each other with 6 to 9 ways while allowing me to slurp the stars from the Yoni-Verse above me.

Be what we are, erotic royalty of soul but touchable bodies of hush.

Plus multiplying the subtraction, of dividing our fraction of lust to love.
Romance it was.

~B.GKL

Chocolate Water 3

Bondage of silk chains for her ankles and wrist, with gold oil drips from a warm copper grail.

Toes of her tired feet swaddled and swarmed by my hand paddled palms, and be gifted with classy bottom taps.

Tongue lubricant of respect oiling the stretch marks of her child bearing hips and glorious restrictions.

Wet natural hair, smiling lips of juicy conversations, and loud mouth camel talk.

Breast of waters falling towards the sheet... what a romantic thought.

~B.GKL

Club Midnight Breeze

As I walk through the foundation.
Of liquored tongues & swaying physical bodies of freedom.

Brainwashed by the scratching
& mixing of rapid vibrations & piercing speakers.

I embrace my rhythm & force my class to present my single strut.

Down to the restroom, thus to drain my inhaled seeker.

As I release my golden essence slowly against the porcelain wall.

In a dripping silence of a water stall.

Licking with vibrations of ignorant bass.

Crooked movement of unrighteous creatures

With a human face.

Pent and bound to emplace.
The frame of mankind.

Living on the edge of empty.
It suddenly still feels crowded.
In club midnight breeze

~B.GKL

Common sense
(Quote)

"The power of the mind!
Is to manifest loyalty to your word!
In which it is bound by your actions."

~B.GKL

Creator Constant

The moment of thinking is dreaming of thoughts; falling towards
an idea uncreated.

The wow that honors your smile with the competition; with getting
it done before the night dream as faded.

Seeing you become the greatest goal to motivating the complex,
through the complicated.
Love your work, and stay activated.

~B.GKL

Creepy Cash
(Quote)

"Money is like bugs crawling around the earth.
It seems to carry many reasons.
Wealth plays a secret tool like insects in life.
Everything has a meaning & a path!
Thus a rule to continue.
The circumstance is what you are made for."

~B.GKL

Cure for loyalty
(Quote)

"Loyalty is like a sickness!
Without it in your life!
It becomes unstable!
Because honor seems to fight as a cure against disloyalty!
To encourage stability & survival in the art of trust."

~B.GKL

Deep Conversation

Can I tell you something?

You don't know me.

Yet I truly don't know you.

So don't try to focus or even try to understand.

My level of respect is made relevant.

Authorizing my spirit, I have to damn shore demanded.

So I will attempt my best efforts to explain.

Overstanding & reaching my altitude of greater success.

I am addicted to moving forward.

It's like a child to a mother's nurturing.

It has a reason to be needed.

Being defeated would never run through my blood.

No matter how much I scuff my sleeping hands.

Not even the alcohol I love.

My drive shall feel this void regardless.

Beyond the darkness, I am commenced to fight through it.
I will see it for what it is.

Who cares about what people think about you or even think about
me?

So forever & then.

In your mind.
Only you can prepare what you need.

With your freedom inside.

You Evaluate & start figuring it out as a child.
Learning through it in your entire life.

Seeing your problems and wanting to run.

People may want to challenge you.

Even if it's family or not.

People will only respect you mostly for what you have.

If you were hungry on the street.

Will you give me food for my stomach?

Only to not feel the grieving.

Regardless of how much stability you have.

You allow clouds over your body to stay warm in anger.

How many tears can you drink overnight?

How many wine bottles can you feel with your doubts?

Because success doesn't work rapidly.

It rarely comes from your dreams.

This is wheeled.

Through patients and existence.
No one is killing anyone's thoughts.
Long nights are where they come from.

Through all the blades.

Facing the shit that I have uncertainly done.

Only to myself over the years.

Suspicious times That I have walked through this world.

Wondering down dark alleys trying to figure it out.

Where will I be in my next breath?

Visualizing myself going somewhere.
Hopefully, my soul will soon agree.

Acknowledging being dark when I want to.

Kissed on the forehead by life or is it death?

Could it be nothing?

We wouldn't care but just set us free.

I can only nurture my comfort.

Stressing to be the man that I need to become.

Just Listen.

Without hesitation.

This is my self-confidence.

My only motivation.

Any & everybody that judge absurdly.
Need's a lot of gossip to be fulfilled.
By opinionating the world.

Never really telling the story about them.

You can't control my status.

You can't tell me what I need to do.

When your pages are not even turning.

You stop writing in your season of chapters.

Because you are content.

In the midst of being in forever limbo.

Looking at all the memories that you have spent.

Redirecting & rewriting old paragraphs just to sound complete.

To figure out.

Whereas my next successful day went.

I am here now.

I'm going over there now.

I see me walking across beaches.

Free & burning in the moon.
No time of night.

Just me & my love.
To say what I feel.

From the tip of my chin.
I know the words I say.
Burning from lips of my tongue like yes.

I can float straight from this window seal.

Far from this deep conversation.

~B.GKL

Driving Too Long

As I Awake.

Driven to drive the untold limitations.

For which my ligaments could not handle.
Muscles put into motility feeling sweat from the rush of
acceleration.

Led foot speeding through life at fragile times.
My eyes have not seen the bounds of sleep.

Creeping pillows of mocking sheep.
Trembling for the rest within me.

How long is the ground of travel?
Rocks and gravel.
Penetrating my hands as it hangs from the car window relaxed.

I can't seem to stop!

I have been going a hundred miles per hour.

With time stuck in seconds per block.

Taking me apart through tunnel vision & blistered feet.
Damn, I've been driving too long.

~B.GKL

Erotic Levels
(Quote)

"A body caressed without fingertips is a sexual soul.
Reaching towards any level of high!
Far beyond a simple tempting thoughts to travel deep.
Gold sweat pierces all realms!
From the glass of her royal cleavage.
Erotic screams banshee through the night.
As her stars give me enchantment forever."

~B.GKL

Essence of Power
(Quote)

"The Essence of power.
Is not caring about having it all!
Yet living it as a natural habit."

~B.GKL

Fireplace Ambers

Trapped calm within soft chambers, of chimney soot, and mental
openness.
Single Peachtree… growling, and thumping with ambers falling.

Overwhelming the blaze by provoking it with needed wood.
Finding relief from the center heat.

What a wonderful fire.
Well, don't you think?

~B.GKL

Flesh & Flame

Scorching heat invades my mind like an oven.

Of the abyss.
I shall make a fist of pain.
Only to create and mislead the flesh of my flame.

What must I gain?
Light through the darkness.
Approaching the structure of my universal gate.

Allowing me to interpret or explain.
I see through the narrow cracks.
Beyond the frozen door.

Searching for immunity.
With the blood of my flesh upon callus hands.

NO FURTHER! (I screamed)
A legion of stars.
Pulling the real me from my hindered bones and brain.

Flesh and flame I feel upon me in the dark of my skin.
Screaming tones disturb the flesh but aware of the soul.
DESCRY!
Peace has arrived.
Flesh from Flame and my soul awake.
Revive me to live for.
Sempiternity I am just!

~B.GKL

Freeing the burden
(Quote)

"As I embrace my morality.
Soulfully drinking the power of my freedom.
Ligaments pushing away the burdens.
Nothing can enslave royalty born without the restraint of
humanity."

~B.GKL

Gaia and Son of Souls

*Gaia: /**guy**-uh: / Mothered Earth*

By all mean thee obedience of thus… which is necessary.
Unfairly shuffles as a deck of cards, and bound as a chest piece of
sacrifices.

~B.GKL

Gain Time

Ceremonial ash plunging towards thee awareness of fading.
Debating against the pressure of time and verbally aging.

Raging within the wisdom that is set forth in contemplating.
Self-invading the power of the minds… one true craving.

To adjust to the need of wanting to know all.
But waiting.

~B.GKL

Gaining Limits
(Quote)

"To fail is to gain success beyond the limits of not failing at all."

~B.GKL

Gems of Gold

My mind should be respected.

From the dirt of my brown feet.

To the top of my spiraling roots.

My walk is the most ultimate class.

It doesn't matter if I am considered rugged.

Rather it's work boots or nice casual suits.

My mind is always maintained.

The success that is nearly exchanged.

By every drop of my storm that I rain.

To show you only how I feel.

I shall gift the dryness of life.

A single thirst.

I am at peace within my spiritual coast.

Do you fathom my well-being?

By standing here in view.

Daydream of me moving forward.
To my lifting my weight in gems of gold.

~B.GKL

Her Deep Formation
Dedicated to my wife: *Charnissa V. Kaigler*

I love you more than the protective veil over my heart.
We move stronger but lighter.
Then the mass of oceans across the earth's backbone.

Our only grievance is that!
Years never brace itself.
For our slow kissing of graceful passion.

Our affection is unseen like hummingbirds feeding.
Truly without harmony in loud destruction & chaos.
My arms buckled around your security.
Guarding the beauty of which you were crafted into immaculate
flavors.

Black cherry's gathered with rosemary.
Gold flakes of amber & chocolate flourish.
Melanin wine.
With a crackle of Solitaires & baguettes.
A combination of beautiful herbs.
Honoring her deep formation.
Become the blue rose from within.

~B.GKL

Hush

Most in this world!
Don't care about your freedom.
All they want to do is control your path and the way that you drive.
The sleepers don't even care if you stay programmed.
Forcing you to learn their stolen knowledge.

They just want you to shut up and close your mouth and try to stay
alive.
Trying to fit in where we don't even need to fit.
This is no comedy.
This is no stage.
This life is no performing bit.

Knock you down and kick you.
Just because they don't want to listen!
Not caring about how free your mind is or the difference you can
make.
Always ignoring the drawings of painting your vision.
Watching you hurting and embracing your pain.
Just wanting a shoulder to lean against.
It surely feels strange.

Every time I come to the center of this window seal.
My whole life is trying to figure out.
What's more important?

Thinking larger or creating a bigger bill.
My debt is within.
Rather I believe in conjuring, meditation, or sin.
My path should be walked alone.
Not without obstacles but not my people.
I love stepping on my feet from a young.
Until I am yet grown!

People in this world think that they are not tools.
To be used.
In the right way to help some!

Get through life.
Easier but only with a graceful hand of caution!
Some people rather judge and control the way that you navigate.
Your mechanical body!

No one wants to inner stand your conscious.
They only want to keep us the same way.
Putting me in the dark closet and trying to hide my power.
I am free.

This is the happiest I have ever been in my life.
Living more diverse!

Including being in a different place!
My motion is unbreakable.
Like the stone peak above a mountain.

I only move when the earth needs me to.
If you'll ever believe it!

The reason why some are refused & considered a black sheep.

Allowing self to do what it wants.
No one controlling the logical mind.

Trust & believe.
Worlds of people throw that family word out there.
That best friend's word!
Out there.

Yet most are not willing to sacrifice anything.
For anybody.
Until the actions are available in their face.

Why should I care what you do?
Why should I give any judgment on how you carry yourself?
Even if it's without peace or with serenity in life.

Who am I to say that you can't do what you are doing?
There is no such thing as good or bad in my eyes, only negative
and positive.
I am free now.
I don't have to listen to anyone but my soul.
So since I've grown & moved on.

I now can see.
How mankind can be so strict?
On the way, you carry your own life.
It's of no importance to you.

So Hush!

~B.GKL

Invincible

Yoni: /yoh-nee/ *the essence of women's universal life-giver and love.*

As I arrive among the morning aggression.
My perception.
Seems to have gained a sentiment position.
Of a profound sequence of sexual incantations.

Shortly she is havoc.
From her feminist agenda.
Waiting to expose my fabric.
To filtrate my body to extreme measurements.
Her Yoni seems to nuisance my wick.
As I shall watch her eyes & body stride in thick.

As her knee's kindled with heat from her inner to her kiss.
Her mind is preparing to liquidate and paralyze.
With an uncontrolled indulgence so organize.
As her nature slowly gained a plan.
To slide my intentions and my hand.

On her back spine.
To the front of her diaphragm.
Love howls like temples of organisms.
Simple minds could never fathom.
The addiction of her fleshly atoms.
So I stand from my center.
I kneeled and handed her to me.
Her smooches upon my hold.
Her reasons calmly inhaling my fantasy making my endurance
invincible.

~B.GKL

Jewels of Fulfillment
(Quote)

"The value of nothing!
As the potential of something!
Feeling an empty abyss with jewels!
Only reveals the growth of fulfillment.
Only an open eye can see.
That it could be full of love.
Never feeding the echoed room is fatal."

~B.GKL

Joyful Silence

It's all up to me to breathe, and release the value of peace while
surrendering my smile to this world.
The gift of just being… has forgiven the hate of just knowing
infinite wondering.

To be one with all parts of what makes me more separately, in
paths my heart as divided.
Sudden emotions of gander and possibilities, sitting against the tide
of my rippling joy!

Happiness clouding the streams of my pain, which once was an
unfiltered feel within me.
New purpose and with a beautiful agenda to seek refuge in the
voids of myself.

Redecorate the temple of ideas, based on old concentration for the
renewal of true focus.
As I stand and face the river fall.
What can I feel?

Nothing but the vibrations of water clashing, and the loud rivers
silencing my worries.
For it is one moment of pure freedom.

~B.GKL

Judge My Crown

Keenng: /kɪŋ/ the truest form of the real King.

Kingdom of my gates.
In relief of my hellish mind.

Hold my hand & take me from my ultimate boil.

Three drops of tears.
Pore from my frontal lobe.
Known as sweat.

Screaming in my mind.
A timeless calling that I pursue.

Alcohol.
On the wounds of my scars.
Placed with no healing to be given.
Do I stop or proceed to find the light?

I have been in solitude.
Hearing the chant of the ancestors singing.
Angry with a tilt of bondage.
My loyalty has been tempted.
Ice in my jaw.

Words of scrolls instilled in my talk.

I cannot drain incessantly
be in frustration.
My foundation.
Is to take the land from my fossil.

Dirt falling from my body.
Constructing my growth.
Why must I?
Entertain my hurry in peace?

Patients to my lock.

To rush is my key.
To be divinity.
Is to fly in my persuasion without shame.
In my rage to revive the serenity within my atoms.

I exchange knowledge from my pen.
Rolling.
My stress against the paper.

Falling I cannot.
I am free from the hell surrounding me.

Boundaries of success to be a Keenng.
Cage walls keeping stories of my future.
Why suffer when a choice is given to the enemy as well as a brother?
Judge My Crown!

~B.GKL

Jungle Nectar
(Quote)
*Gaia: /**guy-uh**: / Mothered Earth*

"The sweetest nectar in this life is entering the waterfall.
Never using an umbrella!
Yet allowing my lust to be washed upon slowly.
Kissing the wound of Gaia through the yoni's power."
Seeking the center of streams!

~B.GKL

Lady in Smoke

Kween: /kwiːn/ *The truest form of the real Queen.*
Yoni: /yoh-nee/ *the essence of women's universal life-giver and love.*
Gawddess: /ˈɡɑː.des/ *Infinite goddess form of a Kween aka Queen in power.*

Sometimes I think people forget about how sweet.
How brown.
How purely in essence it is.
To touch the skin of a melanin Kween!

Let me tell you what her skin is like.
Something more addicted than a dream pipe.

I watched her as she walked across the room.
There's no need to slide any numbers.
On the fact that we are cohesive with one another.

So I look into her eyes.
I felt the depth of one soul.
Feeling her leg cross left…leg cross right!

There's no need to whisper in her ear.
Mumbling passionate things of excitement!
That I have had trapped inside my life.

Baby come here… Come here!
Kween there is no need to fear.

I don't need to drink any Hennessey or beer.
To see your beauty is the essence of truth.

You're so fine, lady.
I can only use my shovel no grind baby.
You can tell me… all then… all lately.
Allow me to bring some pleasure to your environment.
We can grow trees or plants.
We can even do a garden.
Pardon!
My forever absence of my soul.

121

Let me take you in.
When I see you across the room at a table.
You were sitting there gorgeous.
Leg cross left…
Then over your right.
I see you in the mist of the smoke.

I mumbled damn...!
She has to be mine tonight.

You got to see it.
So come on!
Touch the dance floor.
Let me show you how to move across in.

Island to the earth.
You can be an empress but you are my Gawddess.
I hate to be modest.
But…!
I know that your dress is fitting because it is only made for you.

What does it do…? To make you want to turn around.
Slow down… Let me speak us into a dance of silhouette.

I would like to see you in the sunset if we can.
Grab my hand.
It's made of stone but don't be afraid of this.
When I look at you it's like.
Jumping off the end of a cliff into the water.
Knowing that the rocks won't feel sharp.

My love…
When I am kissing you on your lips and hoping that your tongue
doesn't part.
When I grabbed you inside my soul.
I never want to let you go.

The process is available.
Let me show you what it feels like to be married within.

As I bow to a Kween as she dips for me.
She lifts my head from weighing down my shoulders of love.
I'm only telling you how I feel.

So don't push me away.
Let me be at your close distance.

Your lips are like sweet buttery yeses…

Sometimes when I bite your lip.
You bite my lip… I bite your tongue & taste your thigh.
Just to conquer your knees.
Baby the love between our orgasms is the key.

We manifest everything… bringing the love from the astral plane.
Upholding the pleasure that we are going to gain.

Between me and you & the Ankh.
Only makes your Yoni jump.
Can you feel this…!

Spread the clouds.
Open everything that the world doesn't want to do.
Treat our emotions like a shotgun.
Grab it… Shake it.
Rapid rounds of patients.

On the leg… On the bed… On the knee.
What does it matter?
She wants it in the head instead.
Let me tell you where I'm coming from.

It's not always about sex…!
I admire everything about your love and lust.
Anything you have to bring to me next?
I love the times you wake up in the dawning.
You take that single sexy breath.
I like it…!

Your naturalness… Your afro…!
Her afro brushing against my chest.
I love you, Kween.

Allow me to break it down for you.
Slow as it may be.
When I kissed the inside of your in see.
Can you feel it when I let free?

~B.GKL

Letters in One

Letters of duration constrained.
Living our life as a broken Glass & dormant with subtle growth.
Just like the laying of brown clipped grass.

Feeling as if our heart & body is hurting for revenge.
Our sword won't allow us to be great at last.

When you are a human born of fire from this nightmare.

The sensation of running.
Is like a caged but innocent felon.

They tend to grow a new muscle.
In their tongue.
Of truly not giving a damn.

We suffered as one.
Fighting against the submission with rebellion.

Negative entities laugh at our strength.
We are pulled from within to never fall.

Embracing the stones crushing our prideful Back.

Sworn into secrecy to ourselves.
To never resist being stopped.
Towards any painful lack.

Being free in our soul.
Believing the wise owl won't allow us to forget.
That people hate us differently.
More for being more than their equal.
Other than just being facts.

No Matter how much you could love them.
Majority.
Spits in your face just because of the difference.

Don't Crack & won't perm your hair to that straight shellac.
Letters in one wrote from many & that's that.

~B.GKL

Life's Great Theory
(Quote)

"I will rather be together & gone.
Other than alive & apart."

~B.GKL

Long Day at Work

My heart is crawling in my steel toe boots.

Stepping to the pulse of my walk.

For the next shift of repetition.

Clock ticking.
While slaving to the schedule bending my arms.

To watch the seconds betray me.
Minutes & hours are missing.

Gathering my thoughts over loud slashing.
Gritty oil & machines.
Creating distractions as my mental tool is twisting.

Fantasy.

That my clothes are clean & my hands are superb.

When reality kicks in.
I see dirt and stains.
Simply to be washed.

Stomach full of lions & wolves.
Gasping for air.
Growling & snarling against my hungry rumble.

One Crumb to the throat.
Taunting my gut.
To show who's in charge.
Of the wild starving in my digestive bundle.

Always delegated & dragged.
From my deep nodding sleep.

To be pushed into muddy work slacks & worn boots.

Coffee controlling my energy.
Crashing at the end of a cliff.
Only leaving me with nothing but bitter roots.

Dodging through impatient jams.
Engine smoke.
Middle fingers are displayed as kindness.

I guess.
It was just.
Another long day at work

~B.GKL

Lost For Words

My translation.

To spit the product of patients.

Knowledge of inner royalty.

To pass information.
Through symbolic prophets hidden nations.

Allegations.
That my heart is at war.

I creep in flame & become one with the element.

Refusing to heal.
Because I am use to the pain.
Let me explain!
Then become lost for words.

~B.GKL

Love Hold
(Quote)

"Your heart holds no value.
Without placing the priceless love within it."

~B.GKL

Melanin Legs

Sweet legs!

Sweet legs!

The sweetest skin!

Pretty from the bottom of your feet.

To the top of your head.

Sunshine on your melanin.
Then yes!

Cold-blooded you may be.

Blinded in the room of pitch black.

Yet exotic things we still might see.

Do I agree?
That I shall bring.

The passionate temptation to your surrounded avenue.

There is no need to ever be depressed.

Acting like you're down and feeling blue.

I like the way that you twitch.
The way that we invoke our bodies.

Towards the aftermath of lifting off.

When we climb.
Climb & climb.

Climb above the center of the climax.

I can take you on top of the roof.
Fix your shambles.

Clean your gutter.

I can show you what it feels like.

To embrace the old ways.

Take it slow.
Make you butter.
Let me show you what if feels like.

Melanin legs.

~B.GKL

Mental Cage

As I rouse upon this sopping chamber.
Of rusted steel surrounded by loose screws.
With a thousand hunted keys shattered.

Seeing this highly finessed illusion of comfort.
Containing one cot to relax my social imprisonment.
As if it even mattered.

Afraid to scan my perimeter.
I inner stand this metal cage.
Of slightly black scented candles melting in this four to eight
corner silence.

No conclusion.
To lifting the veil of confusion.
Can't explain how I got into this ordeal dealt.
Wounded hand.
When I needed guidance.

My attempt to raze my slump from the springs.
Stabbing my muscle movement of going against the gravity.
Towards the ceiling bars.

I finally made my way to the side.
The raging cot with the potential to criticize my condition.
My energy won't allow my focus mind on the stars.

So I manage to maintain what I felt physically.
Gaining my view of what led me to this wall of rats.
Infested darkness trapped in a Cage.
No time to assume logic.
When I see nothing beyond what I am placed to lie.

Without the thought of escape leaving my heart.

It suddenly feels hard to engage.

Black scented candles ruling the air.
Still unable to see.
Only sounds of this leaking & twisting.

Drops of water tap dance through the corroded bars.
Aside from the steel floor of scattered keys.
Lying everywhere without an exit and a keyhole missing.

Will my mental cage ever decide?
To release what is already free & designed in your choice to walk
out.

Wheeled it.
To drive it into Existence.
No Trap can contain you.

When your eyes are closed but open to the mission.

~B.GKL

Mouth Full of Rain

I cannot.
Inhale or even talk.
When my voice is like cinnamon.
Compact In the back of my throat.

Sun on my lips.
Chipping my brown golden.
Kissable whisperers.
Seeping through my dry yarn.
Shouting to the astral plane.

When my words won't seem to escape my belly.
Feel my chest with so say & say so.
Mouth full of strength.
Wired with an amp but can't create a sound.
Only a tasteless rant bestowed within an entrapment in my ribs.

A closed mouth could never reason with the outside.
Never having to yield to your essence.

Silence is not held within but without.
Meditation is my fuel for speaking to the mind for focus.
So I rest under a broken cloud of rain.
Replenished.

~B.GKL

Music in Poetry

Keenng: /kɪŋ/ *the truest form of the real King.*

The beautiful musical piece that defines the arrangement in poetry.
That arouses the real meaning of peaceful sound.

The elegant aroma that passes the artful feel.
With stanza in my words that touch the sky & ground.

Music in poetry that defeats the motif in versification.
All feels compatible with verbs & nouns.

Meaningful patterns that catch your sound and sight.
Very romantic slowly dramatic both as held the crown.

Many feelings to write and listen so blow the torch.
Snap your fingers yet breathe hissing to my metrical composition.

Every note in both comes motley high in the sky & darkness
through poetry music has risen.

Numerous combinations of melody tunes phrasing many words
With one that alters my vision.

Father rest in peace a strong rider with a soul full of family and the
mind of a musician.

You taught me to never give up, never say goodbye, well Keenng I
shall see you later.

Father, I love you forever until the moon turns clear.

~B.GKL

Poem Dedicated to:
My father Carlos V. Kaigler Sr. 1968-2005

Natural Infernal
Painting By: *Nakessa Simpson*
IG: *@nakdsimpson*
Painting Description: *Original painting colors are red and white.*
Kween: /kwiːn/ *The truest form of the real Queen.*

Earthy, ravishing nappy fury of microphone combustion; brass fist fork picking through the spiral blaze of her feminine power, and hydrocarbon body butter.

Color of ruby kindle flares, and lips of coal coated in cherry crimson carmine puckers; red dress pit containing her chaotic dance.

The romance of ashes, falling slowly from her deep thermal eyes and lashes; batting flames to love letters given to her appetite, with burning arousal of smoke to the sky.

To defy her ambient rings of vapors, and tepid temperature crowding her space would be a freeze without the travel of her motion.

The emotion of her fires casting shadows in the shade, and protection from the hidden values of her blaze; rooted with the blossom of ambers and stones.

Home near your forever warming closeness, of feeding my vision with your taunting but Kween like ways you imply.
Supply me eternally with your natural infernal.

~B.GKL

Now seeing
(Quote)

"A life without disappointments!
Is like falling asleep without the assumption of never waking
again.
It must be! As it is!
To develop a stronger sense of appreciation."

~B.GKL

One Bird above Me

Characters: (The Old Writer: Charles and the Bird: Nylon)
Special thanks for the live narration collaboration, where the bird
was narrated by my talented little sister The Great Writer and
Artist *Nicqua B.* IG: *@NicquaB*, and myself.

Charles Replied:

As I rub the dancing sun from my creative eyes, after a long cricket
like sleep.
All I dreamed about was writing and waking up tomorrow, just to
start on my first book.
With no clue of what it's going to be about... funny right?

But since I am up earlier than normal, I guess I'll soon climb out
onto the rooftop again.
Which is my favorite place to brainstorm the wonders of my
thoughts, on paper.
Minutes after my normal routine of brushing my teeth and so forth!
I grabbed my journal and headed out to the roof of my house...
everyone is motivated in the weirdest places I guess.

As I rise from my window, the mountain air of distant flowers...
slumbers across a warm breeze upon me.
Such a beautiful written welcome I'm sure.

So as I set down and open my notepad, writer's block starts to kick
in and my favorite pen is missing from ear.
I looked around me, and finally spotted my lucky pen; lying on my
bedroom floor near the amethyst lamp.

The only problem is that my window seems to have closed slowly
behind me.
Soundly, I take a couple of breaths just to calm down, and that's
when the small special guest arrived.
One bird above me, lands on the top corner of my house near the
dripping gutter.
Centered perfectly, as it landed in front of this alluring orange fruit
like sunrise.

Dipped blue feathers with a hue of purple and black soft tones.
For some odd reason, I wanted to speak to it.
(Hello pleasant bird from the sky) and nature spoke back softly
but without any mistrust.

The Bird (Nylon) Replied:
Hello Charles… my name is Nylon.
I have been watching for some time now from my oak tree.
I have seen you writing stories of many, but you have never heard
stories of Nylon.
We birds have seen what lies above the minds, of all things that are
fascinating and terrifying.
The tales of what the forest holds as great wisdom and unknown
languages.
Nature as watched its executioners, begin from crawling towards
two legs.
Some destroying all that has been before them and some wish to
love us.
Charles, you seem nervous. Are you ok?

Charles Replied:
I guess I am ok for the most part, just a bit startled as all.
I must say, that you are something extraordinary.
Fore what you're asking of me is a great honor, but how can I
write without my lucky pen and drowning in writer's block?

The Bird (Nylon) Replied:
I shall give you my most superior feather, so that you may conjure
my flight of realistic dreams and travels into elegant calligraphy.
Writer's block will never be a prison ward again for you, but yet a
limitless vacancy of written releases.
I am here to bring you the tales of my gust but given through a
cyclone.

Charles Replied:
Nylon!
Why? Why me?
I am just an old writer stuck on his rooftop with an old notepad!

What gives me the right to unveil your forest of eyes, to countless hearts and some naïve and awake blind?

The Bird (Nylon) Replied:
Well...

My feathers are ruffled and my beak is cracked, but you still only seen my soul in its pure form; without any notice of what I lack in looks.
Your heart was meant to write my legacy.
Charles, that tear that's running down your eye for just gentle me, explains why you must compose my nest of secrets.
My single feather shall write eternally, without the ink of the world but the genealogy of all birds.
Written from the love of your shaking hands.

Charles Replied:
My friend, I agree to be your tool of all life communication without interruption.
My window is also jammed closed, so I humbly didn't have a choice but to hear your chirp.
Beautiful bird, please speak your peace.
My hands are bound to your every remark.

The Bird (Nylon) Replied:
We as birds live to release are young to be strong from the nest, without the fear of depth and height.
While mankind, just hopes that their children can even make it out the front door.
Birds live above and through this world without being judged by the radiance of our feathers.
Most of mankind... kills nature, but the earth always fights back with real earthquakes and brutal storms.
Birds live free until we are enslaved, and forced to carry out messages for war or fly through chemical plants of smoke and envy.
Charles, your heart is good, and you understand that we as birds and animals survive at the top of the food chain.
While mankind is confused about its place!

Charles Replied:

Nylon, please tell me that this history lesson has a happy ending.
My eyes fills with lakes of remorse for your species.
How can I help change the way mankind has twisted the natural way of life?
I am afraid that you may be a bird in need of someone to vent to.
I shall give all my time to you Nylon.
I am different than most.

The Bird (Nylon) Replied:
Well, Charles… sorry to tell you, my friend.
I am much too old to fight in the living, any longer.
My time here with you on this rooftop has motivated me to fly higher into my last existence with joy.
Just having someone, that would listen to an old bird speaking its truth.
That is peace to my soul, knowing that you will protect the earth with just a single feathered pen.
Thank you dearly, and so long Charles…

Charles Replied:
As I watched Nylon, as she vanishes into the orange like sun and cotton poof of clouds.
I smiled deeply with inner standing... that at some point we all get restless and must get free.
Even if it's just venting!
The conversation must have been destiny because my window was fully open when I looked back.
Thank you beautiful bird.
The One bird above me

~B.GKL

Pillow of Roses

Two nectared bodies suckle sweet twisted in bedroom bourbon
fabrics.

Melt against the springs and conjure my entire energy of
commitment.

Interview my soul and recite my fleshly stories and gnawed lips
and dirty dreams.

Cling to our breath and follow the breaks of our air.

Surround our temples with tossed pillows.

Stop time with your smile and random kisses upon my beard.

Chocolate roses drip with body heat and wild intentions.

It's just the way we are.

~B.GKL

Plenty of Time

How long has it been since you've allowed yourself to sit down, and let the sun and sky watch you as you give it the same attention?

Embracing the wind as your lotion, while the stereo of nature plays free melodies; of baby bird chirps and loosely hung chimes.

Tiki torches lighting the grass trim lines, and corners like a legion of fireplace mantles of a peaceful ritual.

A pool of glass waiting for a reflection to disturb its stillness with the dip of a soul.
Sweating glass of beer or sizzling corked bottle of wine to change the element of flavor.

While the sunny glare turns into a late moon glowing like a bowl of milk in the becoming night.
No matter what the ambiance is… always make sure you embrace plenty of time.

~B.GKL

Poetry Bullets

I woke up today.
The same urge to challenge me.
No food in my stomach.
All this knowledge is consumed by my mind.

Belly aching!
Poisonous life without a doctor to assume to take the pain.
Only my self-healing!

Just me alone destroying my humanity.
Killing my feelings.

I am a soul first.
I am not just a man preventing my life into a hearse.

I am always awake.
Against the reflection of myself.
Through the glass of my window watching the sun glare in.
I only can tell you what I feel.
Overstanding where you're going & they're in.

So I looked outside.
I started taking a glance across the land.
Opening my eyes!

Rubbing the pain from my pupil!
My hands are full of sweat.
I am trying to synchronize everything mentally but spiritually.
Through the times of focus.
I'm trying to remember the difference between.
A lucid dream and astral projection.

Within this confusion.
I'm hearing the trees & smelling the bushes full of locust.
Tears running down my flesh yet confused with perspiration.

You wouldn't understand that.

In your life, you may wake up throughout a nightmare.
Sometimes a positive dream could be a trial that you wrecked.

I am only convergent to what my mission is.
My pursuit is to figure out where I place my diamonds.
Fore which I focus on my kids.

That's what I call my motivation of
Knowledge.
Everything that I speak from my mouth.
Yet is manifested without.

I am only trying to tell you where my soul is coming from.
I can't!
I don't have too much trust in my heart.
Unless it's truly the chakra.

It feels like a war on the inside.
When someone feels like they got you.

~B.GKL

Poison Flowers, With Beautiful Hate

The nature of it is evil with touch but remarkable from a distant but
slight nearness of visual sight.
Invite of its tender smell, but toxic center with pollen that is
dreadful towards a random sniff or its aroma in the atmosphere.
Fear of bee stings crowding around this masterpiece of deadly
canvas colors of nature's bucket splashes of rain.

~B.GKL

Reminisce the Present
(Quote)

"We have already been living, but now it's time to live it up… No time to reminisce on what you live."

~B.GKL

Rich Mind
(Quote)

"To be wealthy!
Is not allowing the paper to set the status of your royalty!
Upon counterfeit dreams of using manmade trash!
To pursue a clear path!
Of becoming a raising spiritual gem of having no attachments to greed."

~B.GKL

Screeching tongue
(Quote)

"Being loud & shouting silence in a room full of mirrors!
Only reflects the dynasty of your ignorant tongue.
Hypocritical factions of your weeping voice.
Screaming against the wall to quiet the self-lewdness.
Only you & darkness against the sound of rippling water.
Could create a great solitude."

~B.GKL

Secret Taste

Kween: /kwiːn/ *The truest form of the real Queen.*

Her candy provides sexy toothaches… for my jawbones down the
rhythm of my dull nerves.
Shops of risky nectar, setting the boundaries of my brown lips
upon the melting of hers.

Come forth, to recognizing her aroma that molds my secret
addiction for her grooves and bondage curves.

Fatal flavors of glossy implosion's exploding on my taste buds…
giving her all control and thus.
Sweet tooth, channeling my wants while fusing my needs of swift
intentions… no rush.

Increasing the shakes, for her sugar of smooth and savoring for the
gaze of her liquid paradise, and such.
Wine for the secret taste of a Kween's candy.

~B.GKL

See Me, As Such To Mention

Stand by my heart, and create instruments from my beating metronome.

Smokescreen my visual body, and have a mirage of me as a masterpiece.

Sun gaze in front of my soulful windows and sway with my magnificence.

Solidify your rhythm with my offbeat riff and balance our true maintain.

Struggle to inner stand my instrument and play with my glorious mind.

Secretly become the master.

~B.GKL

Self-Succeed

The powers of my hands.

Reveals the level of my work.

Within the bliss of my carbon palm.

To conjure wars in a silent battle.

Is like a wise whisper.

Among a field of loud enemies to conquer.

Struggling is a way of determination.

Single destinies.

To fore tale future lessons.

Complete or not learned.

From one's mistakes.

To self-succeed.

~B.GKL

Session

We must coalesce as beings driven towards our celestial minds.
For which the human body has small meaning on this level of
touch.

Beauty is an insult to the true meaning of what you are in my eyes.
The way you give my scope a history within the journey of your
open scroll.

~B.GKL

Sir you are all types of crazy
(Horror story: Spoken Word)

As I gather my thoughts.
Walking down this road by myself.
I can foresee myself fading.
Veering off to the side of a ditch.

Then heard a loud noise coming about.
I see an old broken truck from a far.

Dark looking.
Windows tinted.
Painted a very ugly green.

Rusted broken hitch that clicked.
I heard the screws loose inside this piece of crap.

Just lurking along the darkest night.
Looking like something would make me kind of leery.
Of even hitching a ride from this one.

Then I felt myself unwillingly.
Not able to let this one truck just drive on by.
So I felt my hand just stick out.

Out of being eager to get home to safety.
From this weird night of walking.

So I managed to put myself in a situation where.
I am getting picked up by my bad conscience.

It stopped for me.
No words at first.
Just pure creepy silence.

Engine rattling.
Non-cohesive with noise around it.
So I got in.

Barely able to see the face of the driver.
He was like a shadow carrying its heft.
So I continued to look forth and said.
I don't know who you are.
All I am looking for is a ride home.
I feel a bit nervous.
Because I don't normally hitchhike, sir.

So the eyes of this shadowed person.
Looked at me from the side.
It replied in a deep grouchy voice.
(NO PROBLEM GUY)

Then we drove off.

I felt my nerves in my neck.
My sweat running from my face.

Not understanding what I got myself into.

Chewing tobacco all on the floor.
This guy might be hardcore.
Shotgun on the rack.

In the back window with empty shells rolling around.
The only thing I can see is a hat.
Flannel cloths, morose eyes & his murky like skin.
So I tried to remain rivet.
Continuing to keep myself calm.
Thinking to myself.

I know I was lost and needed help.
So I relaxed a little.
I looked at my clock.
I noticed that it was close to 3 AM.

So as this man drove.
Suddenly he spoke again.
Saying in a low tone of voice.

(TONIGHT)
(TONIGHT YOU WILL BE FREE OF MEANING)

I asked why.
He replied quickly.

(LET'S FIND OUT)

He removed his left foot from over the brake.
Jammed the gas paddle down into the floor.
With his muddy boot.

All I can do is grab the door handle and yell loudly.
(MAN STOP, AND LET ME OUT)
Let me out.
I can't die like this.

He replied demonically deep.
(WHO TOLD YOU THAT?
(WHO EVEN GAVE YOU A CHOICE TO MAKE)
(YOU STEPPED IN MY SPACE)
(SO WE ARE GOING TO RIDE THIS ALL THE WAY)
So we drove recklessly ahead.
I blinked and turned to my left.
That man was suddenly gone.
Door wide open with ease.

With no one behind the truck.
The truck was speeding down the dirt road.

The seatbelt jammed and I had nothing to cut it.
Wondering in my mind that nobody can help me now.
Who was that thing or man?
Why couldn't I resist this ride this once?

The truck picked up speed downhill.
I tried to reach the wheel with my left hand.
The steering wheel was locked and the truck raddled like junk.
Black smoke was everywhere.

159

Everything just went to hell.

I tugged the seatbelt once more and it finally released.
I jumped in the driver's seat.
The brakes were out.
The gas paddled was busted.

I'm going a hundred & twenty miles down this rocky gravel.
All I can see is me falling.
Deeper. Deeper. Falling.
Driving into my abyss.
I can only see my world flashing.

I passed out.
Then for some reason, I woke up.
In the same truck but in the passenger seat.
With a tall skinny countryman driving it.

Same hat.
Same flannel.
Different guy.
Then the man spoke to me with an old country accent.
(Hay buddy are you alright)
(I let you in the truck and you seemed out of it)
So I asked.
Man, where am I?

Countryman replied.
(You were hitchhiking on the back roads)
(When you got in you looked a little sick pal)
(You passed out as soon as you got in)
(I couldn't wake you up)
(So I decided to take you to the nearest town)

I replied.
Man, I don't know what happened.
I just had a dream.
A different driver tried to kill me in the same truck.
Countryman replied.

Sir you are all types of crazy.

~B.GKL

Strange Pains

My back hurts with no consent lift.

I've received a terrible but unpleasant gift.

From the cold works & the graveyard bliss.

Wind blowing against my hollow shell.

Seeping.
Into my skin creating agony.

What is my relief towards my strategy?

To stretch my popping joints carelessly but fragilely.

Giving me strange pains.
Migrating through my strong but soft tendons in my torso.

I maintain closer.
To my organs as it attacks itself.
I have given it my all.
Prescribed to grow weary of ache & torture.

~B.GKL

Sweet Drums

Death flea's far from manifestation.
Inner standing that our natural nature is spiritually existing.

Without any assistants.
Of suicidal aura of mental commitment's.

To help us physically expire in thought.
Beyond all earthly conditions.

Of secret pain & illusions of peaceful conviction's.

As the eye box of snakes.
Try to melt immoral waves upon our true status & vision.

To force us to believe that the artificial is the true prediction.

Of our higher self.
The false heritage of intruders.
Planning to never allow the full masses to listen to reason.

Using the third eye tongue.
To remain us as one.

The plot is set for our demise.
They implant lies through our daughter's womb
& enjoy our son's labor when they are young.

Turning them against the natural law of manifesting greatness.
Death is an illusion to the ear and eyes.
When life on the terrain is among.

As the mystical skirmish is here-there-and from.

Fire burst with passion for swords & sum.
Silent but rapid with sweet drums.

~B.GKL

The Aurora of Her up Rise
Keenng: /kɪŋ/ the truest form of the real King.

Her smile.
Her voice. Her mind. Her glow.

Rising above the mattress of silk sheets.

The way she yarns when looking into the sunrise.

Beautiful toes sliding in her slippers.

She is golden when her hair is natural.

Come to me.

I see you as you beautify yourself.

Before you reflect in the mirror.

You are already divine.

You are royalty along with being mine.

You are only meant for a Keenng.

No other.
Could hold your structure.
You're ambiance.

Your body speaks volumes of many words.
In many shapes.
You are very melodic.

You are the tonic that heals my herbal sickness.
Just from licking your lips.

The way.
You look at me in my third eye.

164

The way.
Exotic languages roll from your whispers.

Be my day to day surprises.
Just vibe with me.

So upon the rise of the dawning.
I know that you will shine.

I love your love in the morn.
It's like a phoenix flocking its wings.
From a volcano of flames.

Memorizing like a candle.
Melting off the side of a dresser.

Showing me.
That this love is unique in so many forms.

Forming deepness inside.

The aurora of her up rise.

~B.GKL

The Enchantment of Life

Kween: /kwiːn/ *The truest form of the real Queen.*

Love enchants my life.
Relief of a Kween to blow hollow kisses & repair my broken heart
twice.
Heated stones melted in her passion like chains with ice.

She is gifted as a royal deity & revealing the dawn of life.
She enchants my distance with oils and cream.

My temptation for love boils as I mark my fingerprints of passion
in her steam.
Connected with cherries rolling down as I graze her unseen.
What love seems to mean.
To turn light into murkiness.
Within our shadows.
I reach the tip of her rose sweeping petals between.
Words touch her needs with spoken words of my therapy.
Slowly riding the sunshine into dark blinds of jazz to seem.

Clouds drop! Flowers rise!
Her rose and my black passion in tops.
With rainy tears that surrounds the moaning vibes.
Waterfalls would fall.
With tears in the sun's eclipse with her brown eyes.
Truth intake lies upon the enchantment of our life.

~B.GKL

The Infinite Mind of Lio'lf
"The Poet B.GKL/Brotha GKL/ Gawd Keenng Lio'lf"
Pronunciation- [Gawd-King-Lah-If]

Spoken Word

I am ***Lio'lf***, which is not life but more of infinite thinking without boundaries constraining the forest like the mind of my mental totem… the lion and wolf; hunting my subconscious thoughts like prey, to be consumed and reborn as interminable cerebration.

Ruling the mental mansion of cabinets weighed down with scattered files, just holding my entire moments of over inhabited ideas waiting to be scripted or written; watching the heartbeat of my lion and wolf-like ego becoming aware of their kindred purpose.

Grasping the endless degree of never determining any form of limits or rules to what information is given from the brain to the mouth, and the hand; to speak it, and recited from the magnitude of numerous view locations and dateless brainstorming.

The essence of the lion oversees the pride of many works while observing the bigger threat of protecting the multifold of interpretations; the essence of the wolf aligns the pack of dreams to maintain the territorial mortality of the poetic craft and principle.

I am *Lio'lf*!

The center of my kingdom and nature, with the state of mind to always live inside out my head; overstanding that the mind is infinite by the soul, and promises are predictable and broken by the flesh... for yet being so defective but a useful tool.

Turning all pain into soup with a glass spoon of anticipation towards the hot cup of tea of forlornness; hoping to wipe away isolation with a napkin of consequences, walking away from a chair of change and the table of contemplating out the house of my reality door of past tense.

I am not a *Keenng* because of worship, entitlement, and jewels upon a throne; yet I am royal because I conquered my fears of not surviving the sword that I've placed in my own heart at times of adolescence.

Guided gracefully by some and misled gracelessly by many, soon taking mental responsibility for the choices of life's enticements; being influenced by the subconscious heart to follow the simple impulses, while then breaking my own.

For I am *Lio'lf* now, a continuous uninterrupted being, damning my flaws every second this clock of lies presents time to me; opposite paws of two leaders clawing through my two-sided temple protecting the new me, in which they have formed from within.

Protecting me insanely while in the plane of the jungle brush, while hiding my hurt and anger built from my beautiful three seeds being separated from me; by the thorns of debt and three tainted bellies that carried pawn holding agendas after the water broke upon the firmament.

I will never live to perish, but I shall only live and exist, *Lio'lf* is what I am!

The meaning of true depth while breaking all attachments and labors of human control and say so, I am bonded with what has no fatigue but understands its worth.

Being that nothing is more individually valuable, other than choices buried far within me… to convey my divine imagination while speaking with consistent logic upon making self.

I carry no expanse, I am *Lio'lf*… walking with my decisions, wolves howling, and lions growling, centered in my skull of what I was born to be.

I am *G.A.W.D,* grand ambidextrous wordsmith developer; forming my head into language and law of my designs crafted from every part of my thinking process and living, no longer in need of nurturing when I have finally gained *The Infinite Mind Of Lio'lf…* which is three of me in sync.

Gawd Keenng Lio'lf… lion and wolf!

~B.GKL

The Marriage in My Words

Gawddess: /ˈɡɑː.des/ *Infinite goddess form of a Kween aka Queen in power.*

What is marriage in my thought & mind?

It is yet defined as two perfect souls.

Meant only for one another.

Only casting perfection.
In both their eyes as one union.

Her soft nurturing skin is like burning sand.

Beneath a single river's palm tree.

Her lips are calm.
Her body moves with the ray of the sun.

A Gawddess is what she is.
Part of this world but divided.

She is sweeter than the petals falling at an altar to vow.
Only to love her dearly.

Marriage to me is like a strong attraction you get.

When you are afraid of something so potent.
Although worth it.
Can't you hear?
The marriage in my words.

~B.GKL

170

The Patches of war

Parallel natures of war reaching its existence.
The warmth of mental peace is vandalized within its conditions.
Calvary with blistered hands of damaged visuals.

Miserable factions to see it for what it is.
Broken models of manmade shelter in a fizz.

Unforgivable... forced into livable pain to turn face.
Poverty becoming the normality of militant greed.

Tears of wine only soothe the drunken world's frustration to bleed.

~B.GKL

The Tantrum Room

Unzipped.

Black ripped jeans.

With her favorite loose shirt.

Showing me that it's only.

Winter cold beneath the panting her exhale.

Soft breast crowning.

Beautiful dotted Prints of her innocent attentions.

My view is chained to her bondage.

She grasps very tightly.

In that vibrant leather pose.

Complements of her gorgeous presence.

Addicted to her lusting rage.

The tantrum room is consuming me.

~B.GKL

The Union

My mentality is a garden for my soul.

Barefoot energy walking across roots, and growth.

Tending to the purpose of me, and my crown… to give me shade
from the cosmos.

The universe can sometimes be overbearing and blinding.

Even for a soul of pure golden ratios.

The flesh is a part of my lower self.

Always acknowledge the freedom upon fresh dirt.
What are we?

A union!

~B.GKL

The Voice Gate of Her

Erotic channels, of her throat gambling moans of screaming or
whispering love again.

Beautiful tones of earth sounds, stroking the back of her lathering
palate to speak.

Gracefully utter words of potent sweetness from the pudge of your
golden stretch marks.

Free your indigenous rage upon my clever forest excursion to seek
your adventure.

The affinity of our enigmatic engagement is prophetic upon the
novelty to be spellbound.

The spawn from my root chakra, to the womb of your chambered
gut; and celestial creations.

Let's watch sage cremated to blown dust, and candles melted to
mellow mush like mercy.

Earthly love is a common impostor, and haze compared to the
hearth between our infinity fires.

So let me hear the voice of your gates… and release.

~B.GKL

The World Tag

Keenng*: /kɪŋ/ the truest form of the real King.*
Gaia-tize*: /guy-uh: tize/ Mothered and one with the earth.*

Suit and tie twisted.
Ballistic!

Animalistic, growls of brown tone honey; reminiscing thee existed.
Fluorescent bright, cinnamon poteen eyes.

Candy carbon silhouette!
Dressed with nothing but Gaiatize.

Her mind is sleepy, rest you're pineal and voice your opinions
towards my zip.
Saliva thickens weakly to confess your Nile, and testify my phallus
with whipped.

Cream… of dreams circulated blossom of streams.
I am a world tag, romancer, and Keenng.

Split her creative love, and respect the life of her seasonal springs.
I am The World Tag, of all mental erotic dreams.

~B.GKL

Thoughts

As I set upon this bus.
My mind has lost the ability to see.

Why is time so short?
Is it allowing me a moment to breathe?
Hours vanished.

Survival instincts allowing me.
Limited ways to bleed.
With the body, heart & mind.
Blind!

With a randomly pure soul.
That temps to read.
We are here for our last days.
Without any instantaneous way to leave.

Misled by the program that takes what we achieve.
We give too much.
With less time to receive.
In heated blood of refuge.

Torched memories set to freeze.

To see liars lacking a legion of moral souls to believe.
All we can do is look in the mirror.
Reflecting our higher selves.
As I doze into a trance, conjuring the sheep.
Somebody wants us gone.
How could this be?

No one else but the one that plots to speak.
Much heart & no guts to eat.

Soldier open your vision.
Durability is to be applied in the weak.
So yet you run for what?

You should stand your ground.
Even if.
The scorching burn of the jungle holds your feet.

Suicide does not construct all victims to leap.

It's the flaw of some humankind.
Criticizing & wrongly competing.

With the lost & the poor.
Because they are not so perfectly neat.

What makes the rich so damn complete?

Just my thoughts.

~B.GKL

Thriving Yoni

Yoni: /yoh-nee/ *the essence of women's universal life-giver and love.*
Gaia*: /**guy**-uh: / Mothered Earth*

Panties clinched.
Into a deep valley of maple brown.

The shore among traveling is dormant.
In the crevices upon the peacocking camel's toe.

A glare of vehemence.
Pushing soft water from the skin.
To replenish the scalding insertion.
Of the sun's flow.

Humps & camber.
Empowering the distance of long trotting.
Across Gaia's bending back.

Taking no brakes.
Wiping the honey from your lips.
After a fresh bite of beehives coax.
On the travel of moist tracks.
Sun is gone.
Now the moon.
Coming about over a mountain of thriving yoni vibrating the trees.

~B.GKL

Total Strength

It takes a divine gamble
To truly withstand.
The strength of long-suffering demands.

Although.
Pleasing the world with open hands.

To be humble only to fathom life's plan.

One day.
Spreading remains across the northern land.
Time being valued upon a kingdom's nest.

Through the weakest moments before life had begun to climax at
its best.

The strength of power was slightly designed & compressed.

Within the red blaze of orange inflamed threads around the vest.

Craters erupt with aggressive force into a peaceful rest.
With skills of life gained in portions.

As the world waits for equanimity upon a place of thought.

Sleepless dreams.
As sunny days weep the drifting pulse.
Summers stay warm.
As winters grow frost.
Pain is no more.
The dreadful nights are lost.

As well as debt as no limit.
The reason is no cost.

Freedom from the present that we all have known.

New limits of sound performing a fair well song.
Silence freeing the mind before the vitals are gone.

Total strength carries on.

~B.GKL

Traveling Mind

I have been troubled by the innocent matter.

Circulating wine drunken from glass & shattered.

Is it a fact that I am unseen?
Between the ripples of horrific dreams.

Implanting the damaged & inflamed patterns.
Through currents of water.
With divine secrets of planets unknown.

Let me take my time.
To travel through my astral plane
& convey the thin lines.

Between lies that are redefined.
As a traveling mind.

My feet mean nothing.

~B.GKL

Twelve Chambers of Solitude

One determination to reverse this single gavel, from slamming
down on my soul with restraints!
Two mental complaints of why and how, with a reserved
discomfort… waiting to place my mistakes on a steel cot!

Three years of sweat, anger, and repent, fueling my freedom but
always welcomed with the same cold bars.

Four birds cross above the yard, over a wall… I was unable to see
the other side of the earth; I'm sure they landed.

Five hundred demanded attempts, I tried to just deal with my time
sentenced, while the pen of life keeps rewriting my novel.

Six to 10 reps on the bench, trying to ignore the wars, and gangs
crossing hands to do what all hustlers would.

Seven years of lights out… well my pen writes my passage, while
the moonlight is used to see my creation.

Eight days after last year, with the same old brawls and fights,
mean mugs and threats, with no worries here.

Nine to twenty pages wrote, with a feeling of maybe I'll see thee
outside once more, as a man of change.

Ten guards and maybe a riot seem to be brewing again, for the
same old reasons for releasing frustration.

Eleven years before I see my possibility, of seeing my freedom,
my desire, and my motivation, to conquer those past years.
Twelve chambers of solitude, with my heart on a manuscript and
my soul being the concrete of liberation.
The patients of twelve chambers of solitude, imprisoned within
with a hand full of keys.

~B.GKL

Unforgettable Love

Walking waters of cement layers and currents of waves feuding.

Enchanting but dangerous depths of pressure; squeezing the sands glass.

Distant winds of mental findings, brewing the sea chills of my soul search.

Gazing upon the far-out seeing's, of clouds comforting the sun's seating.

What am I stating?

The idea of freedom and nature; making unforgettable love!

~B.GKL

Untitled

Rest your hands upon the shoulders of my aura and read my higher intentions.

Allow your crown to lean against my intellect, creating our empire of mentions.

Achieving the greatest touch of sensual aggression through numb bitten lips!

Moaning is a clinch, towards the level of tones we create between our gifts.

Drifting and entwined in our cocoon of bamboo sheets and perfectly twisted.

Mystic words of self-control, conjuring the mojo's goal to magically visit!

No need for candles when we bear the light in this romantic darkening.

Sparkling love we manifest in shape from realms the bodies carpentering.

She climbs my tree for my maple to utilize the fruit of our labor.

Fill your belly with my majestic love.

~B.GKL

What Is Love?

Most of humankind forgets.
That they ask so many simple questions.
Unanswered.
What is it? Love!
What does it mean? How to care for it?

Love wakes up in the dawning.
Besides the mountains in the corners of her eye.
With a hundred dragons beyond her smile.
With a sweet kiss to take the waste away.

What is love?
Love is when your car is broken.
Yet being able to put her on your back.
Saddling her up to which she deserves to be.
Above the mind.

What is love?

Love has no limit on pleasured pain.
No matter how many footsteps.
As laid over your heart.
Nothing comes before your diamond in her temple.

What is love?
Love is the process of making yourself available.
Towards everything emotional.
No matter how soft.
How tight it is.
Around my masculine glove.
What is love?

Love is the essence.
Of something that you are never able to handle.
Yet curious to figure it out… the purpose.
Only the sacrifice of what you are willing to risk.

What is love?
Love is when you are so high strong but sensual.
As two entities.
We can lay down our vital force.
Slowly silhouetting.
Into a great submission of vibrations.

What is love?
No matter how strong or how high.
That your crown may rise above the sealing.
You will never forget the love.
That is under your shoulders.

What is love?
I guess it's just something I love.
When she kisses me.
Goosebumps run across my neck.
With a slight touch.
Of her soft breast pressing against the wings around my spine.
What is love?
Just Us!

~B.GKL

Why This Why Us

Although.
Ripping her clothes would be truly juvenile.
Both hands.
Of comforting volcano's
Fabric melting.
Beneath the succulent ways of her Nile.
Like fruits from the abounded throat.
Passages.
Which we thrust for one love.
Why this? Why us?

~B.GKL

Women Abused by Domestic Love
Kween: /kwiːn/ *The truest form of the real Queen.*
Spoken Word Short Story

She is battered… bruised… scarred, smite; by the hands of her husband's use, and controlled by a man that forever provides abuse.

Consumed by whatever frustrates the mental mind of the masculine energy within this man that I would consider a punk.

Blunt in his nature, taking his anguish of anger out on his Kween… she has become suppressed; forced to submit to these great pains of power… above her flesh.

She pushes emotion from her gut to tell him that she still loves him, followed by yet another single strike to the face… next.

He oddly caresses her body and then knocks her between two chairs to rest.
The best sleep that she has ever gotten was a concussion while beaten and criticized for nothing.

Chiseled down as something that she was not purposely trying to go into, but only falling in between the verge of finding love.

She is misused and torn and dragged through the entire house.
Eye, face, mouth… focus loss and pushed out of cars upon 66 routes, spontaneous slaps slashed across the face in a car from the driver's seat.

She already feels it coming, she foresees the anger and frustration in his face; she's just waiting on the anticipation of when his hand and her face shall meet.

Being a custom to it, being keen to now knowing when it's time for a random beating to come for her at any time of the day; wondering in her mind, can this man hear her thoughts… *SLAPPED* subconsciously for what she feels on the inside about this man that acts like an angry but weak boy. Wondering how she could ever have considered him a husband, a boyfriend, a best friend, or even a man.

She feels that she has to stay there, unable… wobbling legs weak and can't stand while incapable to demand the one question… why are you beating me?

She couldn't see it at the altar while wearing her beautiful dress, seeing him clean and pressed… down to the bottom of his dress shoes with the grooms and the bridesmaids.

But as soon as you were mentally there to see the real him, you were already being torn down to nothing; beautiful smile traveling towards his fist, his kick, his boot… he comes home from work drunk and roaring because he lost another job while losing all of his loot to motel affairs and then taking it out on you.

So many strangers with children have witnessed the publicly brutal scenes, of all the outrageous beatings of distress and swelling of the eye; sometimes you were wishing you could take your life and die, but you can't even cry as the head wound bleeds and runs down your tears.

What it means my Kween it doesn't matter what people say, I ask you to please just leave… you can escape; Be free from the torment, tyrannical times waking up in the morning… your cooked breakfast consistently decorating the walls because he is angry every dawning.

Becoming more wrathful without warning, mourning the day that you ever met this man; your high school sweetheart has grown to be just like his father, and his grandfather… ripping the smile from the soul of whom they love completely apart.

You've never seen it, punched eyes, screams of hollering cries… dragged and pulled across what was home with rug burns on the body because he won't respect you.

Every time that he lay's his hands on you, all he does is reflect the same trauma that he has seen done to his mother and sisters; sometimes it's just in him to be that way, just like any other programmed and abused by another.

He starts repeating one of his dead quotes, *"baby I'm sorry… I only do it because I love you… I promise I won't do it again"* and begins to web spin you another lie, like putting a fish on a hook and keep you in constant rotation while watching you revolve without end.

Smacked across the room through five racks through a den, head pushed through the glass and then another dead quote was spoken *"baby I love you… we can win"*; face, eyes again followed blow to the chin, and broken down to her being placed back into the hospital trying to survive… contemplating to stay alive.

People say that there is a thin line between love and hate, when did they ever get to love to prove rather that's what it is; where is the thin line where it doesn't hurt?

YOU DON'T HAVE TO STAY!

Do not live as someone's punching bag or a counterpart of a fake champion practicing his self-fight on your face.

*Look at you, look at you, look at you…*You think you can love him, and still have hate for his battling hands.

Sometimes it's hard for someone to be a superhero for you, because when I risk my life and take this man down… you will run to protect your abuser while questioning the hero *(why did you hurt him?)* You will protect your abuser before you protect yourself.
WALK AWAY!

Every single opportunity he had, he would verbally abuse you in front of your friends; your friends whisper in your head, asking you why you deal with this suffering.

She would always say I don't know with excuses; he doesn't mean to… while constantly making up more reasons to not leave a coward that loves hurting your being; there is no excuse for any man to lay hands on a woman, let alone a woman enticing a man to hit her to make him look sinister to the world.

This is not just one of many cases… It's all, but why fall in love to be broken and constantly have to keep shoveling your wonderful pieces together?

Depressed, and weeping every night while calling your mother on a phone; telling her more harmful things about what is going on in your life, and feeling that no one wants to protect you.

Death has become your motivation, but you are unable to detach yourself from the situation. You're used to it being this way basically, the lovemaking that you now have feels like you are being raped by your love because all the abuse turned you numb.

While you lay there being embraced, and he feels like he's making love to you as he sweats over you with belt buckles hitting the bedboard like shackles… you begin to scream into your head to become a bird.

The only thing that comes to your mind just makes *it stop…* with you hoping the next time he hits you; the blow takes you out and just ends it all instead of you having to do it yourself.

Ending your life is never worth it… ***JUST LEAVE!***
Nothing was holding you there but your thought of fear, you are free to disappear into a new life with one that loves you.

There are people out there that will help you, that weakness that beats you is not a man nor a boy; what he is… is vermin, so escape from his filth and let it consume itself in its unworthy ways.

Remember he only hurts you because he has already become an unfixable problem because when a real man hits a man and hits a woman, that vermin becomes a faint disappearing stench.
I ask you to leave… just leave, because a man that hits a woman is afraid to hit a real man or just sick for abusing what he claims he loves.

~B.GKL

Wondering Soul Hands

Kween: /kwiːn/ *The truest form of the real Queen.*

Her nervous knees and back heels engraving its already scuffed
timbered floors.

Hands locked to lap, showing the first signs of never being
erotically broken.

Gold glitter melted to her shoulders, with the scent of shea butter
running from her flesh.

Trembling bosoms, while the yoni is sweltering and preserved
beneath her irritable patience for my plans.

Black fitted sundress, exquisite curves imprinting the edge of my
sand bed.

Commando Kween without lingerie and sitting as if it's truly
relished marvelously.

Superb is what I have known, hence the past tense yoga dinners
with her torso, and thighs.

She has always been such a lady, the way her calf muscles crosses
behind my neck.

But furthermore, my wandering soul hands shall relax her needs.

The love that I am for her… Is Infinite.
~B.GKL

Written Letter to Ms. Karma
Spoken Word

Dear, Ms. Karma

Why do you stand us up so drastically at the table of slender hopes, leaving us in an unsocial knowing of rather you're even aware of what has been or what we all are going through; providing us with another one of your many empty seats unfilled, while we continue to place our anguish of unjustified torture in the anticipation of seeing a proper occurrence?

The assurance in your ability as weakened rapidly in our eyes as we feel what you ignore as the disaffection settles within us all, the way that you have become numb to the smell of flaring night lights hanging and burning from broken branches; does the sound of a house vacant of any hero around to defend the child touched without an ear to protect their words, but unknowingly weeping for you to give them vengeance and become their true adjudicator.

You always seem to come later or just late to make such pains so minor, without any real penalty towards a human with a piranhas appetite, can you at least make sense of this realm of illusion that most are afraid to leave when its time; where the hell are you when a woman's jaw becomes a man's way to relieve his brute stress of life or to control her because his soul is weak, where are you when a woman provokes a good man to become a raged animal just to be a victim to the world… caged or shot like a hunters wooded catch of any day.

Are we forced to just lay and wait for Ms. Karma to correct the lies and stolen truths that need real revealing of historic faces changed and broken to match the identity of what oppresses most of us still? We are tired of you not showing up when justice is not giving anyone justice and just killing the world in the sight of the world, why don't you give this planet of all pestiferous souls a torment as they have never bared? Compared to all that we can, and cannot see, we often wonder will the hands that break the world down into an unforgettable exertion feel much worse of what they have engraved in the hearts of so many tears.

As people disappear, and nutrients are made more toxic while television programs entertain more fabrication until mankind sees it as ok but uncomfortable; jobs made into chains of metal rings keeping you from a true self career of knowing your abilities, and nine to five's become the new plantation for your soul as schools become the newly adopted parents for your child's mind and the way they should think. While people sink, Karma where is your need and power to somehow show us redemption, we feel no exemption from the things that want us to have an early demise; we realize nothing changes overnight but can be made more delightful with a schedule of your time being interfered by our complaints of what is vengeful or not.

Can't you see that the earth now feels like a shiny apple that rots over and over with the help of what needs it to live… racism, wars, separation, and greed; so many desires to control what deserves to stay free, without the worry of being taken from its family and used for all agendas of what some of mankind thinks is important.

Ms. Karma, I only ask what is soulfully possible in what is needed, we desire a true restart on all things unbalanced; revenge from us would be childlike, so we await the karma towards the menacing deeds at hand. Ms. Karma, please read my letter with time but with haste.

Sincerely, *The Poet B.GKL*

Yoni of Crowns 1

Yoni: /yoh-nee/ *the essence of women's universal life-giver and love.*

Strong soft tip against the cerebellum!
Tempting to persuade the womb of creation.
Yoni of great acceptance upon a spontaneous moment.

Allowing the plate to be cleaned from the vocal of each grunt and
moan.
Phallus taking a break… to allow the tongue to proceed with
consistency.

Allowing her frequency to refill the cosmos within me.
Taking in her nectarous value and honoring her cinnamon
estrogen.

To be continued… because the inner verse is endless.

~B.GKL

Yoni of Crowns 2

Yoni: /yoh-nee/ *the essence of women's universal life-giver and love.*

Inner versed and tangles, within the Yoni of endless travel.

Prowling through jungle sheets, of bamboo silk… swaddling our animus ways.

Slow, scaturient waters; fall from the souls of us… welded in subtlety.

The crown of her slit smile overwhelms the juncture; we have placed in the honorable entrance.

Receive the key to my adherence, and allow me, the meridian.

Break my body with your demented moments, of wild candy.

The Yoni of crowns makes the darkness seem luminous.

~B.GKL

You're Sweet Shots in the forest

Gawddess*: /ˈgɑː.des/ Infinite goddess form of a Kween aka Queen in power.*

Be my cognac...
Wine dipped within addictions of brandy's firmament.
Trap me in the borders of your open doors and sealed upon the
shut.
Lay your finger upon the center of my rambling unawareness.
Exchanging our hunger through soft but solemn body language.
Revealing the hidden surface of your appealing permanent marks.
Fingertips drifting down the tree roots of your hips.
Your Body is engraved with the barrens of your womanly oath.

Seeking her sweet shots of insanity.
Within the forest that I have been laced.
Yet losing my mind within her beautiful ways.
Seeing the conditions of our love excel through our changing
faces.

Be my compass and magnetize the range of my scope.
Bite the flavors of my heart and free my bitter past.
The taste of our carnal zest cures the moment.
Majestic Gawddess please enjoy my soul as it attains.
Secret entry.

I desire no freedom from your ancient entrapment.
I came to seek the acquired blend of body bath and herbs.
Purge my honor and make me immortal in chaos.
Read my body with the lick of your slithering gap and hiss.
The rise of your Kundalini stands coiled at the arch of your spine.
So, let me see the command of your harmony.
Seeing the wilderness utilized at the base of your evolution.
Rivers drinking sweet shots in the forest of her appetite.

~B.GKL

Your Supreme Word Conjurer Is Here
Spoken Word

As I take the simple text and strain the simplex genre from its sentence while twisting the words to become what I command… other than using ironed out words for a paper that is meant to eat vocabulary with a pencil led that makes it feel wrinkled and gritty sometimes.

Dictionary enslaved to my bidding, presenting me with the most optimum way to transfer my steeping outside the cookie-cutter box, just to challenge any title and make complex easily sound, and interwoven to become the same.

Thesaurus turning love to emotion, hate to detest, and fortune to circumstances; conjuring words to conspire with sound and video communication, making (to, too and two) echo like the mathematic obligation of six when it's different but caressed and identical.

Mastering the speech of hidden language through poet rhythms, with spoken word guidance… with a candy smell of stories being unwrapped into a sweet tooth of many; the remarkable ways my words are conjured from the blaze of my core, through the streams of bass chords.

Conjuring lyric of defined definition, and giving it the feeling to shout from the most secret places within my head of textual matter; allowing the lines to conflict and dispute against the sentences of deranged ideas to make words speak my terminology.

Burning pages of my old poems over a candle of renewal to watch my words ignite over my eyes while watching the wind read the pages of my past thoughts; reading the last page as it burns away in my hand with a subtle blow to the universe.

Engraving so much energy into what isn't written against the tree turned to paper; using my words to water the thirst of what shall be painted ink forever.

I am the rumble of storms gifted with the lexicon built in the soul of my three fingers, the thumb, index, and middle finger holds on to the pen strokes to paint my world; I conjured all words the world shall read from the tears my late hour eyes.

My nature is to bring words from my body and teach me to walk through life in place of myself after I am put to rest to perform for the universe as an old soul.

I shall walk to the stage of all the stars and speak out loud to say, *"Your Supreme Word Conjurer Is Here"*.

~B.GKL

WELCOME TO,
The Serenaders Lounge...
THE ARTIST SPOT LIGHT PRESENTS
Dawn Michelle

Before you begin to turn this page to read **Dawn Michelle's** beautiful words, which introduce her mind of who she has become and the depth of who she is. I want to acknowledge and give thanks to my family **Dawn** for being such an awesome sister and best friend to me, and such incredible support as well as a talented writer that I love and enjoy collaborating with. The consistency in her pen has crafted such beauty in all styles of writing; we are a true team when it comes to continuous short stories and more. I would like my sister to end my book for me, by presenting her walk and who she is as a strong being and a powerful melanin woman. I love you for always being a great sister that I am happy to call family, now let's turn the page and respect the words from one of many wonderful writer's.

Dawn Michelle
IG: @dawnmichellepoetry

I am the Dawn.
My name means to begin anew.
So many circumstances tried to drown me.
Attempting to change my point of view.

Bitterness couldn't consume me nor take root in my heart.
My foundation is too strong to ever part ways.

Infused in strength and resilience is my middle name.
Royalty that is me it's the lineage from whence I came.

Face set like a flint carried me through many storms.
Protected and shielded when evil tried to cause harm.

A Queen nurturing as a garden planted in fertile soil.
Speaking life to a King, my prayers be the wind at his back.
So that he can walk on air knowing that he too is royal.

I am a woman with ample abilities.
Life tried to dim my shine but bright remains in my personality.
Tender heart yet tough as nails in strength and articulated
disposition.
Meek in spirit but don't get it twisted.

My vernacular is well versed in warfare tactics.
Once I open my mouth your ending may be tragic.
Crawling on your knees in imminent defeat.

Return to sender.
Never underestimate what is perceived to be of gentle gender.
Mother of a Queen and three Kings.

Royal Dynasty we are.
Sister to a King and two Queens.
Forever family.

Gifted to give and seldom to take.
Multiplicity is in my hands.
A generous and fruitful soul.
Favor follows me wherever I stand.

Teacher to those willing to glean of the wisdom I impart.
Forgiveness keeps me in forwarding motion.
While gratefulness flows from my heart.

My battle wounds may show but I am a consistent conqueror.
Yes, I make mistakes, at times, for I live outside of my comfort
zone.
It may appear as if I'm by myself please trust.

I am never alone.
Given the prognosis of 30 days to live at birth.
Purpose caused me to look in the mirror.

Experience spoke to me of my worth.
Gifted with insight when I listen.

Determined to walk the path I was given.
I will never declare defeat.

Though there are no visible signs of the way life previously
handled me.

Positivity is what fuels me.
I am truly the rose that broke through the concrete.

By *Dawn Michelle*

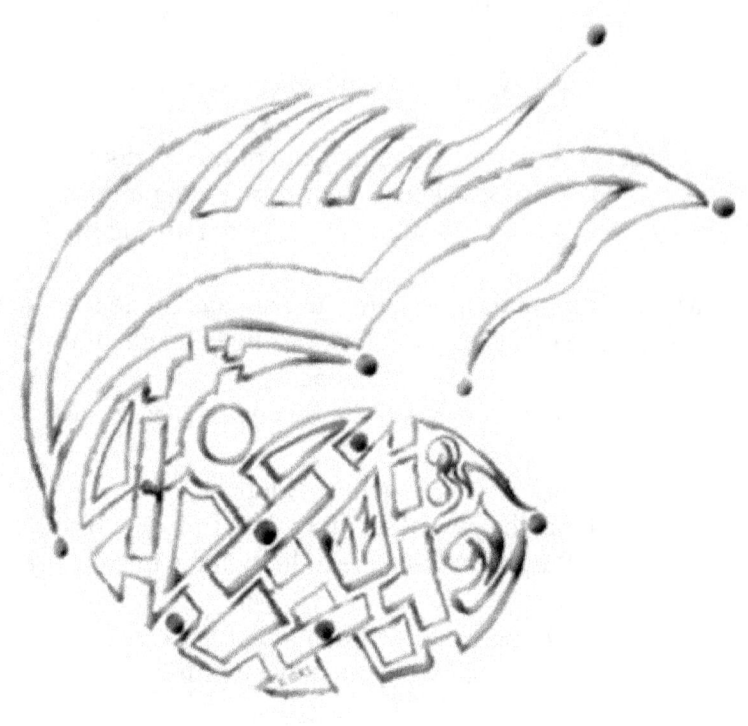

"The Cahnubus of 13"
Pronunciation- *[Cah-New-Bus]*

Art by **Gawd Keenng Lio'lf**
Pronunciation- *[Gawd-King-Lah-If]*

#676

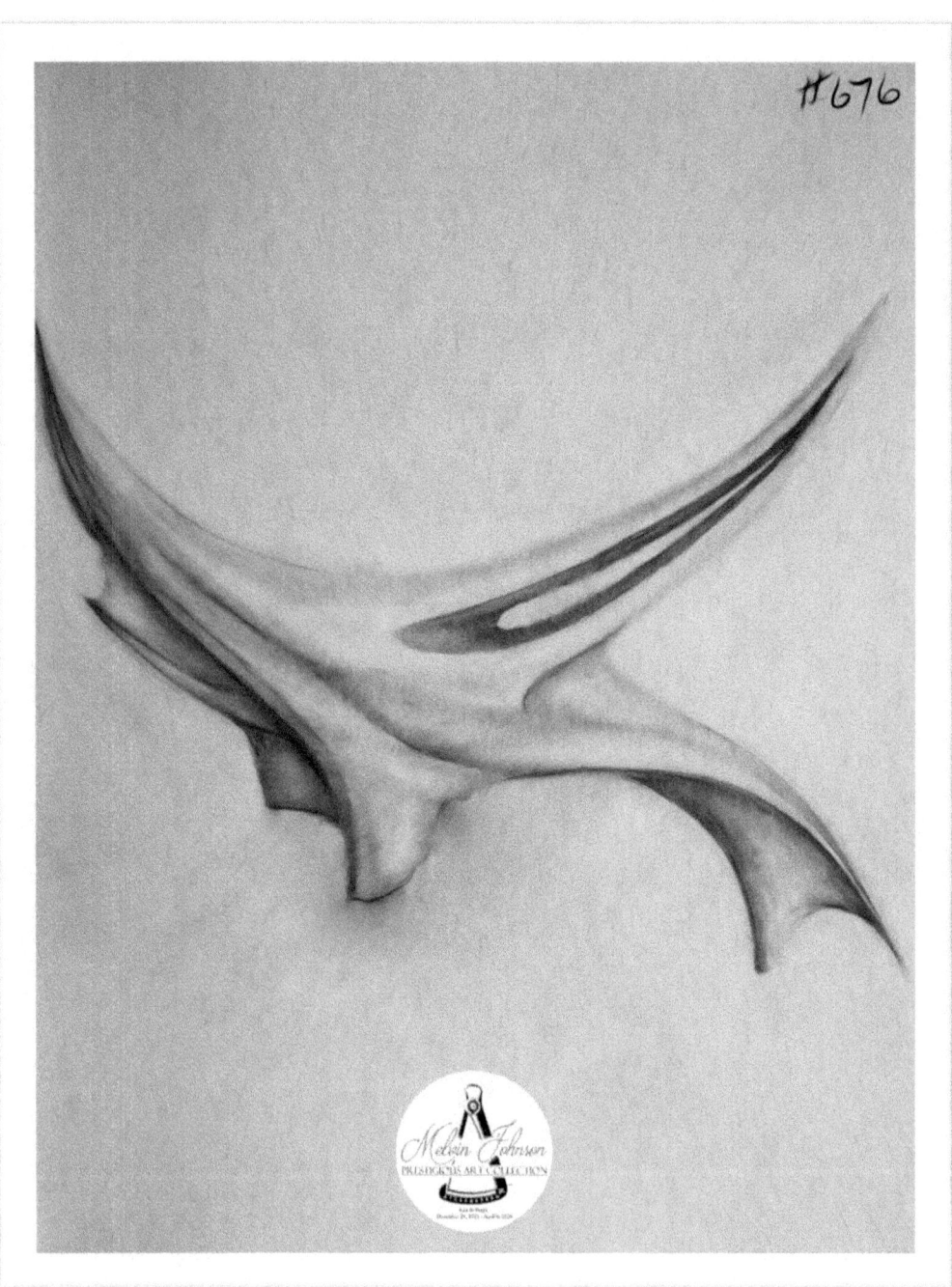

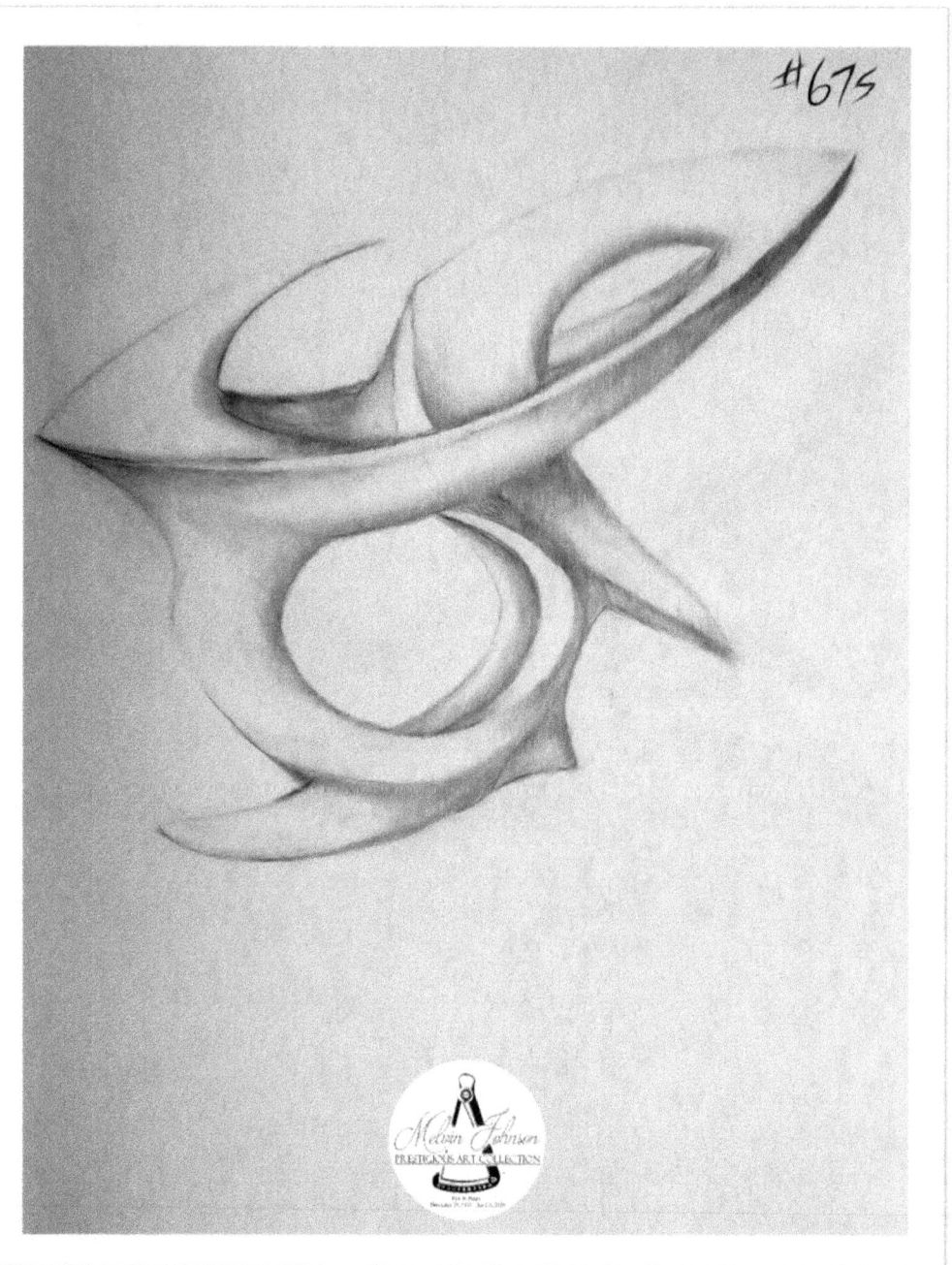

207

#674

Author The Poet B.GKL

I was born on December 28, 1986, and raised in Detroit, MI. I have always been most known for being a multi-talented triple threat when it comes to entertainment. Being able to switch from Hip Hop, Neo-Soul & R&B, and never forgetting to be the pure poetic writer that I have grown to become. I am a black hole of hidden artistry, and I take glory in all the crafts I hold with a humble hand of strength.

My main goal is to build, network, and collaborate with unique talents from all races of people, and bring different minds together to create incredible short stories and art; my biggest skill is bringing anything I write or do to life while breaking the boundaries of all writing limits.

Sincerely, *The Poet B.GKL* aka *Brotha GKL/Gawd Keenng Lio'lf*

Professional: Writer, Author, Poet, Narrator, Graphic Designer, Photographer, Videographer & Audio Editor, Script Writer, Actor, Artist Developer, Motivational Speaker, Ghost Writer, Social Media Marketer, Neo-Soul Singer, Hip Hop Artist, Studio Recording Engineer, and Model.

Website:
www.authorbgkl.com

Sites:
https://linktr.ee/Thepoet_BrothaGKL
https://linktr.ee/MrAndMrsKaigler
https://linktr.ee/CvaughnKphotography

Email:
Thepoet-b.gkl@hotmail.com

Business:
C'vaughn'K Graphic Designs
(313) 334-9630